TALES
from
TIMES PAST

I had a little Nut tree,
Nothing would it bear,
But a   silver nutmeg
And a   golden pear

TALES
from
TIMES PAST

Edited by
Bryan Holme

A Studio Book
The Viking Press · New York

To Elfrida

First published in 1977 by The Viking Press
625 Madison Avenue, New York, N.Y. 10022

Published simultaneously in Canada by
Penguin Books Canada Limited

Library of Congress Cataloging in Publication Data
Main entry under title:
Tales from times past.
  (A Studio book)
  SUMMARY: A collection of fairy tales, fables,
and rhymes illustrated by well-known illustrators.
  1. Fairy tales. (1. Fairy tales. 2. Fables.
3. Nursery rhymes) I. Holme, Bryan, 1913—
PZ8.T149   398.2   77-4665
ISBN 0-670-69159-3

Printed in Japan

Title page illustration by Eleanor Vere Boyle from "A New Child's-Play" (1877).

Contents

The song of the early birds.

In Fairyland

Introduction • Illustrations by Richard Doyle

Once upon a time, after fairy-story hour was over, children went to bed by candlelight, and in the morning they awoke under a soundless sky. The quiet outdoors might be disturbed by the rustling of the trees in the wind, perhaps, or the chatter of the birds—little else. Men were harnessing the horse, not steam or electricity in those days; and the sounds they knew had changed little, if at all, since the very first cock crowed at dawn.

Even as late as the 1820s (when Grimm's fairy tales were first being read in English) had anyone been told that darkness might be turned into light by the mere flick of an "electric"

7

switch, likely he would have shaken his head and smiled—about as delightfully impossible an idea, surely, as Cinderella's Godmother wishing a pumpkin into a coach of gold!

Nor, in the thousands of years since Icarus tried out those fatal wings of wax and plunged to his death in the blue of the Aegean, had anyone seriously thought that man would fly, until in the present century of scientific wonders—as if by magic—this happened too.

Swifter than the Swallow that carried Thumbelina on his back to the far-away island in the sun, swifter than any bird or beast had travelled before, man's noisy metal monster of the sky remained his newest of wonders until time and familiarity made the aeroplane, like his every other invention, a wonder no more.

A dream comes true and the magic departs, so it is said, like the fairies who:

With deeds well done,
Made quiet in their soft-petalled beds till break of day
When all were gone
Before the dew drops fell—carrying magic o'er the way.

Triumphal march of the Elf-King.

While the mysteries of nature have preoccupied the philosopher and sage in their quest for life's meaning, the scientist has been tempted to bend nature to his will, the artist to portray it, and the poet to interpret it by allowing his imagination the most extravagant flights of fancy.

Through poetic imagery, ancient beliefs and superstitions developed into myths: those symbolic tales of gods and heroes wherein heavenly creatures, to satisfy some worldly whim,

8

would descend effortlessly to earth in the guise of humans or animals, and earthly creatures, to achieve some heroic ambition, would have to fight for it—usually at fearful cost. Mountain, ravine, torrent, or raging sea might block the hero's path; strange monsters of the air or deep loom menacingly before him. Gorgon, dragon, giant, witch, sorcerer, thief, or knave—one, perhaps all, must be vanquished "ere the treasure—or the hand of the maiden fair—be gained."

From the same colourful sources the more popular tradition of the fairy story developed: the shorter, less harrowing, simpler tale for children that came more quickly to the point and was acted out on a smaller stage. To no one's surprise, characters would often turn out to be animals who spoke and behaved like humans—horribly like them at times, as Little Red Riding Hood, for one, found out.

Each fairy-tale plot provided adventure and surprise; each theme a strong undercurrent of mystery and romance, lending to the whole a magic aura of enchantment which, when the story drew to a close, left the listener, or reader, longing for more.

Through the centuries the classic fairy stories have been told and retold, with few changes— a cut made here, an irresistible exaggeration lengthening it there—as one generation passed a

familiar tale on to the next. Early descriptions have pictured children gathered round the hearth with the family on a cold winter's evening to be filled with warmth, to listen, to wonder. What magic might the fairies, the witches, or trolls have been up to today, what prince turned to frog, what beast turned to prince, what princess will step into the fairy chariot and be drawn by butterflies across the skies to that land where everyone lives happily ever after?

9

Flirting.

I know a present she will prize—
A team of spot-winged butterflies,
Right in flight; or else with ease
Winding through the tops of trees
Or soaring in the Summer sky.

The Prince travelled from a far country that he might place his
crown at her feet; while offering her his heart and his hand.

Most people say that "Cinderella" has always been their favorite fairy story. Probably it is the most romantic of all the great classics, with the possible exception of "Sleeping Beauty." It is also the oldest. Some authorities claim that parents were telling an early version of "Cinderella" to children in China a thousand and more years ago.

Although younger, "Sleeping Beauty" and "Puss in Boots" were both being referred to as "ancient stories" in 1697, when the Frenchman Charles Perrault decided to take quill firmly in hand and commit these and six other favorites, including "Cinderella," to paper once and for all. And so, with the words set down and printed, the fairy tale became literature.

Other writers were to compile other collections, notably the Comtesse d'Aulnoy, soon after Perrault; Jeanne Marie Leprince de Beaumont, late in the eighteenth century; and the Grimm Brothers, Jacob and Wilhelm, early in the nineteenth. In the 1840s, in Denmark, Hans Christian Andersen was writing his own original fairy stories; in the 1880s, in America, Howard Pyle was illustrating many books for children, and writing some himself; and in 1888 England's Oscar Wilde, an author all too often overlooked in the field, gave to the world *The Happy Prince and Other Tales,* a collection of some of the most poignant little stories ever written. By then books illustrated by Walter Crane, Kate Greenaway, and Randolph Caldecott were all the rage and the golden age of illustrated classics was reaching its height.

Contributing, from the beginning, to that golden age had been the Victorian taste for romantic literature and art, the prosperity of the average family, and the increasing number of children who, those hundred or so years before television became a nursery world unto itself, found reading most enjoyable, and the best of the indoor pastimes—except, perhaps, for watching a "magic lantern" show—that their parents approved.

It also happened that faster printing presses were making books less expensive to produce, cheaper to buy, and, therefore, more widely read. Toward the end of the nineteenth century, and into the early twentieth, the vast improvement in commercial colour reproduction was put to increasingly good use in the new illustrated editions of Grimm, Andersen, Perrault, and other collections to which such artists as Arthur Rackham, Harry Clarke, Kay Nielsen, and Edmund Dulac were to contribute their skills. Especially lovely were the bindings in which the colour illustrations were hand-tipped onto heavy tinted paper. These first printings, or "gift" editions, while prized by collectors today for technical reasons, quality of illustration, and rarity, naturally were originally bought as much or more for the familiar stories themselves.

At best, what the well-written, well-illustrated fairy tale can offer is enchantment, a poetic idea that can lift the human spirit above the "dailiness" of a humdrum world, lend wings to the inventive mind, and encourage the universal desire for the new, the interesting, and the beautiful to happen.

The tales that follow, and the pictures accompanying them—all created by the dozen or so major artists working from the 1850s until shortly after World War I, by which time the light of the golden age of elegance had already dimmed—are presented with enchantment uppermost in mind. On the preceding pages, for example, the scenes and captions taken from Richard Doyle's large portfolio "In Fairyland," published with a poem by William Allingham in 1870. Merely to look at these pictures is enough to give most people, as they enter a completely different world, the happiest kind of feeling. And that is the book's intent.

Thumbelina

Hans Christian Andersen • Illustrated by Eleanor Vere Boyle

There was once a woman who wanted to have a tiny, little child, but she did not know where to get one from. So one day she went to an old Witch and said to her, "I should so much like to have a tiny, little child; can you tell me where I can get one?"

"Oh, we have just got one ready!" said the Witch. "Here is a barley-corn for you, but it's not the kind the farmer sows in his field, or feeds the cocks and hens with, I can tell you. Put it in a flowerpot, and then you will see something happen."

"Oh, thank you!" said the woman, and gave the Witch a shilling, for that was what it cost. Then she went home and planted the barley-corn; immediately there grew out of it a large and beautiful flower, which looked like a tulip, but the petals were tightly closed as if it were still only a bud.

"What a beautiful flower!" exclaimed the woman, and she kissed the red and yellow petals; but as she kissed them the flower burst open. It was a real tulip, such as one can see any day; but in the middle of the blossom, on the green velvety petals, sat a little girl, quite tiny, trim, and pretty. She was scarcely half a thumb in height, so they called her Thumbelina. An elegant polished walnut-shell served Thumbelina as a cradle, the blue petals of a violet were her mattress, and a rose-leaf her coverlid. There she lay at night, but in the day-time she used to play about on the table; here the woman had put a bowl, surrounded by a ring of flowers, with their stalks in water, in the middle of which floated a great tulip petal, and on this Thumbelina sat, and sailed from one side of the bowl to the other, rowing herself with two white horse-hairs for oars. It was such a pretty sight! She could sing, too, with a voice more soft and sweet than had ever been heard before.

One night, when she was lying in her pretty little bed, an old Toad crept in through a broken pane in the window. She was very ugly, clumsy, and clammy; she hopped onto the table where Thumbelina lay asleep under the red rose-leaf.

"This would make a beautiful wife for my son," said the Toad, taking up the walnut-shell, with Thumbelina inside, and hopping with it through the window into the garden.

There flowed a great wide stream, with slippery and marshy banks; here the Toad lived with her son. Ugh! How ugly and clammy he was, just like his mother! "Croak, croak, croak!" was all he could say when he saw the pretty little girl in the walnut-shell.

"Don't talk so loud, or you'll wake her," said the old Toad. "She might escape us even now; she is as light as a feather. We will put her at once on a broad water-lily leaf in the stream. That will be quite an island for her; she is so small and light. She can't run away from us there, whilst we are preparing the guest-chamber under the marsh where she shall live."

Outside in the brook grew many water-lilies, with broad green leaves, which looked as if they were swimming about on the water. The leaf farthest away was the largest, and to this the old Toad swam with Thumbelina in her walnut-shell.

The tiny Thumbelina woke up very early in the morning, and when she saw where she was she began to cry bitterly; for on every side of the great green leaf was water, and she could not get to the land.

The old Toad was down under the marsh, decorating her room with rushes and yellow marigold leaves to make it very grand for her new daughter-in-law; then she swam out with her ugly son to the leaf where Thumbelina lay. She wanted to fetch the pretty cradle to put it into her room before Thumbelina herself came there. The old Toad bowed low in the water before her, and said: "Here is my son; you shall marry him, and live in great magnificence down under the marsh."

"Croak, croak, croak!" was all that the son could say. Then they took the neat little cradle and swam away with it; but Thumbelina sat alone on the great green leaf and wept, for she did not want to live with the clammy Toad, or marry her ugly son. The little fishes swimming about under the water had seen the Toad quite plainly, and heard what she had said; so they put up their heads to see the little girl. When they saw her, they thought her so pretty that they were very sorry she should go down with the ugly Toad to live. No; that must not happen. They assembled in the water round the green stalk which supported the leaf on which she was sitting, and nibbled the stem in two. Away floated the leaf down the stream, bearing Thumbelina far beyond the reach of the Toad.

On she sailed past several towns, and the little birds sitting in the bushes saw her, and sang, "What a pretty little girl!" The leaf floated farther and farther away; thus Thumbelina left her native land.

A beautiful Butterfly fluttered above her, and at last settled on the leaf. Thumbelina pleased him, and she, too, was delighted, for now the toads could not reach her, and it was so beautiful where she was travelling; the sun shone on the water and made it sparkle like the brightest silver. She took off her sash, and tied one end round the Butterfly; the other end she fastened to the leaf, so that now it glided along with her faster than ever.

A great Cockchafer came flying past; he caught sight of Thumbelina, and in a moment had put his arms round her slender waist, and had flown off with her to a tree. The green leaf floated away down the stream, and the Butterfly with it, for he was fastened to the leaf and could not get loose from it. Oh, dear! How terrified poor little Thumbelina was when the Cockchafer flew off with her to the tree! But she was especially distressed on the beautiful white Butterfly's account, as she had tied him fast, so that if he could not get away he must starve to death. But the Cockchafer did not trouble himself about that; he sat down with her on a large green leaf, gave her the honey out of the flowers to eat, and told her that she was very pretty, although she wasn't in the least like a Cockchafer. Later on, all the other Cockchafers who lived in the same tree came to pay calls; they examined Thumbelina closely, and remarked, "Why, she has only two legs! How miserable!"

"She has no feelers!" cried another.

"How ugly she is!" said all the lady chafers—and yet Thumbelina was really very pretty.

The Cockchafer who had stolen her knew this very well; but when he heard all the ladies saying she was ugly, he began to think so too, and would not keep her; she might go wherever she liked. So he flew down from the tree with her and put her on a daisy. There she sat and wept because she was so ugly that the Cockchafer would have nothing to do with her; and yet she was the most beautiful creature imaginable, so soft and delicate, like the loveliest rose-leaf.

The whole summer poor little Thumbelina lived alone in the great wood. She plaited a bed for herself of blades of grass, and hung it up under a clover-leaf, so that she was protected from the

A beautiful Butterfly fluttered above
her, and at last settled on the leaf.

14

rain; she gathered honey from the flowers for food, and drank the dew on the leaves every morning. Thus the summer and autumn passed, but then came winter—the long, cold winter. All the birds who had sung so sweetly about her had flown away; the trees shed their leaves, the flowers died; the great clover-leaf under which she had lived curled up, and nothing remained of it but the withered stalk. She was terribly cold, for her clothes were ragged, and she herself was so small and thin. Poor little Thumbelina! She would surely be frozen to death. It began to snow, and every snow-flake that fell on her was to her as a whole shovelful thrown on one of us, for we are so big, and she was only an inch high. She wrapt herself round in a dead leaf, but it was torn in the middle and gave her no warmth; she was trembling with cold.

Just outside the wood where she was now living lay a great corn-field. But the corn had been gone a long time; only the dry, bare stubble was left standing in the frozen ground. This made a forest for her to wander about in. All at once she came across the door of a Field-Mouse, who had a little hole under a corn-stalk. There the Mouse lived warm and snug, with a store-room full of corn, a splendid kitchen and dining-room. Poor little Thumbelina went up to the door and begged for a little piece of barley, for she had not had anything to eat for the last two days.

"Poor little creature!" said the Field-Mouse, for she was a kind-hearted old thing at heart. "Come into my warm room and have some dinner with me."

As Thumbelina pleased her, she said: "As far as I am concerned you may spend the winter with me; but you must keep my room clean and tidy, and tell me stories, for I like stories very much."

And Thumbelina did all that the kind old Field-Mouse asked, and did it remarkably well too.

"Now I am expecting a visitor," said the Field-Mouse; "my neighbour comes to call on me once a week. He is in better circumstances than I am, has great, big rooms, and wears a fine black-velvet coat. If you could only marry him, you would be well provided for. But he is blind. You must tell him all the prettiest stories you know."

But Thumbelina did not trouble her head about him, for he was only a Mole. He came and paid them a visit in his black-velvet coat.

"He is so rich and so accomplished," the Field-Mouse told her. "His house is twenty times larger than mine; he possesses great knowledge, but he cannot bear the sun and the beautiful flowers, and speaks slightingly of them, for he has never seen them."

Thumbelina had to sing to him, so she sang "Lady-bird, lady-bird, fly away home!" and other songs so prettily that the Mole fell in love with her; but he did not say anything, he was a very cautious man. A short time before he had dug a long passage through the ground from his own house to that of his neighbour; in this he gave the Field-Mouse and Thumbelina permission to walk as often as they liked. But he begged them not to be afraid of the dead bird that lay in the passage. It was a real bird with beak and feathers, and must have died a little time ago, and now laid buried just where he had made his tunnel. The Mole took a piece of rotten wood in his mouth, for that glows like fire in the dark, and went in front, lighting them through the long dark passage. When they came to the place where the dead bird lay, the Mole put his broad nose against the ceiling and pushed a hole through, so that the day-light could shine down. In the middle of the path lay a dead Swallow, his pretty wings pressed close to his sides, his claws and head drawn under his feathers; the poor bird had evidently died of cold. Thumbelina was very sorry, for she was very fond of all little birds; they had sung and twittered so beautifully to her all through the summer. But the Mole kicked him with his bandy legs and said:

"Now he can't sing any more! It must be very miserable to be a little bird! I'm thankful that none of my little children are; birds always starve in winter."

"Yes, you speak like a sensible man," said the Field-Mouse. "What has a bird, in spite of all his singing, in the winter-time? He must starve and freeze, and that must be very pleasant for him, I must say!"

Thumbelina did not say anything; but when the other two had passed on, she bent down to the bird, brushed aside the feathers from his head, and kissed his closed eyes gently. Perhaps it was he that sang to me so prettily in the summer, she thought. How much pleasure he did give me, dear little bird!

The Mole closed up the hole again which let in the light, and then escorted the ladies home. But Thumbelina could not sleep that night; so she got out of bed, and plaited a great big blanket of straw, and carried it off, and spread it over the dead bird, and piled upon it thistle-down as soft as cotton-wool, which she had found in the Field-Mouse's room, so that the poor little thing should lie warmly buried.

"Farewell, pretty little bird!" she said. "Farewell, and thank you for your beautiful songs in the summer, when the trees were green, and the sun shone down warmly on us!" Then she laid her head against the bird's heart. But the bird was not dead; he had been frozen, but now that she had warmed him, he was coming to life again.

In autumn the swallows fly away to foreign lands; but there are some who are late in starting, and then they get so cold that they drop down as if dead, and the snow comes and covers them over.

Thumbelina trembled, she was so frightened; for the bird was very large in comparison with herself—only an inch high. But she took courage, piled up the down more closely over the poor Swallow, fetched her own coverlid, and laid it over his head.

Next night she crept out again to him. There he was alive, but very weak; he could only open his eyes for a moment and look at Thumbelina, who was standing in front of him with a piece of rotten wood in her hand, for she had no other lantern.

"Thank you, pretty little child!" said the Swallow to her. "I am so beautifully warm! Soon I shall regain my strength, and then I shall be able to fly out again into the warm sunshine."

"Oh," she said, "it is very cold outside; it is snowing and freezing! Stay in your warm bed; I will take care of you!"

Then she brought him water in a petal, which he drank, after which he related to her how he had torn one of his wings on a bramble, so that he could not fly as fast as the other swallows, who had flown far away to warmer lands. So at last he had dropped down exhausted, and then he could remember no more. The whole winter he remained down there, and Thumbelina looked after him and nursed him tenderly. Neither the Mole nor the Field-Mouse learnt anything of this, for they could not bear the poor Swallow.

When the spring came, and the sun warmed the earth again, the Swallow said farewell to Thumbelina, who opened the hole in the roof for him which the Mole had made. The sun shone brightly down upon her, and the Swallow asked her if she would go with him; she could sit upon his back. Thumbelina wanted very much to fly far away into the green wood, but she knew that the old Field-Mouse would be sad if she ran away. "No, I mustn't come!" she said.

"Farewell, dear good little girl!" said the Swallow, and flew off into the sunshine. Thumbelina gazed after him with the tears standing in her eyes, for she was very fond of the Swallow.

"Tweet, tweet!" sang the bird, and flew into the green wood. Thumbelina was very unhappy. She was not allowed to go out into the warm sunshine. The corn which had been sowed in the field over the Field-Mouse's home grew up high into the air, and made a thick forest for the poor little girl, who was only an inch high.

"Now you are to be a bride, Thumbelina," said the Field-Mouse, "for our neighbour has

17

proposed for you! What a piece of fortune for a poor child like you! Now you must set to work at your linen for your dowry, for nothing must be lacking if you are to become the wife of our neighbour, the Mole!"

Thumbelina had to spin all day long, and every evening the Mole visited her, and told her that when the summer was over the sun would not shine so hot; now it was burning the earth as hard as a stone. Yes, when the summer had passed, they would keep the wedding.

But she was not all pleased about it, for she did not like the stupid Mole. Every morning when the sun was rising, and every evening when it was setting, she would steal out of the house-door, and when the breeze parted the ears of corn so that she could see the blue sky through them, she thought how bright and beautiful it must be outside, and longed to see her dear Swallow again. But he never came; no doubt he had flown away far into the great green wood.

By the autumn Thumbelina had finished the dowry.

"In four weeks you will be married!" said the Field-Mouse. "Don't be obstinate, or I shall bite you with my sharp white teeth! You will get a fine husband! The King himself has not such a velvet coat. His store-room and cellar are full, and you should be thankful for that."

Well, the wedding-day arrived. The Mole had come to fetch Thumbelina to live with him deep down under the ground, never to come out into the warm sun again, for that was what he didn't like. The poor little girl was very sad; for now she must say good-bye to the beautiful sun.

"Farewell, bright sun!" she cried, stretching out her arms towards it, and taking another step outside the house; for now the corn had been reaped, and only the dry stubble was left standing. "Farewell, farewell!" she said, and put her arms round a little red flower that grew there. "Give my love to the dear Swallow when you see him!"

"Tweet, tweet!" sounded in her ear all at once. She looked up. There was the Swallow flying past! As soon as he saw Thumbelina, he was very glad. She told him how unwilling she was to marry the ugly Mole, as then she had to live underground where the sun never shone, and she could not help bursting into tears.

"The cold winter is coming now," said the Swallow. "I must fly away to warmer lands; will you come with me? You can sit on my back, and we will fly far away from the ugly Mole and his dark house, over the mountains, to the warm countries where the sun shines more brightly than here, where it is always summer, and there are always beautiful flowers. Do come with me, dear little Thumbelina, who saved my life when I lay frozen in the dark tunnel!"

"Yes, I will go with you," said Thumbelina, and got on the Swallow's back, with her feet on one of his outstretched wings. Up he flew into the air, over woods and seas, over the great mountains where the snow is always lying. And if she was cold, she crept under his warm feathers, only keeping her little head out to admire all the beautiful things in the world beneath. At last they came to warm lands; there the sun was brighter, the sky seemed twice as high, and in the hedges hung the finest green and purple grapes; in the woods grew oranges and lemons; the air was scented with myrtle and mint, and on the roads were pretty little children running about and playing with great gorgeous butterflies. But the Swallow flew on farther, and it became more and more beautiful. Under the most spendid green trees beside a blue lake stood a glittering white marble castle. Vines hung about the high pillars; there were many swallows' nests, and in one of these lived the Swallow.

"Here is my house!" said he. "But it won't do for you to live with me; I am not tidy enough to please you. Find a home for yourself in one of the lovely flowers that grow down there; now I will set you down, and you can do whatever you like."

"That will be splendid!" said she, clapping her little hands.

There lay a great white marble column which had fallen to the ground and broken into three

The Swallow flew down with Thumbelina, and set her upon one of the broad leaves.

pieces, but between these grew the most beautiful white flowers. The Swallow flew down with Thumbelina, and set her upon one of the broad leaves. But there, to her astonishment, she found a tiny little man sitting in the middle of the flower, as white and transparent as if he were made of glass; he had the prettiest golden crown on his head, and the most beautiful wings on his shoulders; he himself was no bigger than Thumbelina. He was the spirit of the flower. In each blossom there dwelt a tiny man or woman; but this one was the King over the others.

"How handsome he is!" whispered Thumbelina to the Swallow.

The little Prince was very much frightened at the Swallow, for in comparison with one so tiny as himself he seemed a giant. But when he saw Thumbelina, he was delighted, for she was the most beautiful girl he had even seen. So he took his golden crown from off his head and put it on hers, asking her her name, and if she would be his wife, and then she would be Queen of all the flowers. Yes! He was a different kind of husband from the son of the Toad and the Mole with the black-velvet coat. So she said "Yes" to the noble Prince. And out of each flower came a lady and gentleman, each so tiny and pretty that it was a pleasure to see them. Each brought Thumbelina a present, but the best of all was a beautiful pair of wings which were fastened on to her back, and now she too could fly from flower to flower. They all wished her joy, and the Swallow sat above in his nest and sang the wedding march, and that he did as well as he could; but he was sad because he was very fond of Thumbelina and did not want to be separated from her.

"You shall not be called Thumbelina!" said the spirit of the flower to her. "That is an ugly name, and you are much too pretty for that. We will call you May Blossom."

"Farewell, farewell!" said the little Swallow with a heavy heart, and flew away to farther lands, far, far away, right back to Denmark. There he had a little nest above a window, where his wife lived, who can tell fairy stories. "Tweet, tweet!" he sang to her. And that is the way we *learnt the whole story.*

Puss in Boots

Charles Perrault • Illustrated by Gustave Doré

A Miller, dying, divided all his property among his three children. This was a very simple matter, as he had nothing to leave but his mill, his ass, and his cat; so he made no will, and called in no lawyer, who would probably have taken a large slice out of these poor possessions. The eldest son took the mill, the second the ass, while the third was obliged to content himself with the cat, at which he grumbled very much. "My brothers," said he, "by putting their property together, may gain an honest livelihood; but there is nothing left for me except to die of hunger—unless, indeed, I were to kill my cat and eat him, and make a coat out of his skin, which would be very scanty clothing."

The cat, who heard the young man talking to himself, sat up on his four paws, and looking at him with a grave and wise air, said, "Master, I think you had better not kill me; I shall be much more useful to you alive."

"How so?" asked his master.

"You have but to give me a sack, and a pair of boots such as gentlemen wear when they go shooting, and you will find you are not so ill off as you suppose."

Now, though the young Miller did not much depend upon the cat's words, still he thought it rather surprising that a cat should speak at all. And he had before now seen him show so much adroitness and cleverness in catching rats and mice that it seemed advisable to trust him a little further; especially as, poor young fellow! he had nobody else to trust.

When the cat got his boots, he drew them on with a grand air, and slinging his sack over his shoulder, and drawing the cords of it round his neck, he marched bravely to a rabbit warren hard by, with which he was well acquainted. Then, putting some bran and lettuces into his bag, and stretching himself out beside it as if he were dead, he waited till some fine fat young rabbit, ignorant of the wickedness and deceit of the world, should peer into the sack to eat the food that was inside. This happened very shortly, for there are plenty of foolish young rabbits in every warren; and when one of them, who really was a splendid fat fellow, put his head inside, Master Puss drew the cords immediately, and took him and killed him without mercy. Then, very proud of his prey, he decided to go directly up to the palace, where he begged to speak with the King. He was desired to ascend to the apartment of His Majesty, where, making a low bow, he said:

"Sire, here is a magnificent rabbit, killed in the warren which belongs to my lord the Marquis of Carabas, which he has desired me to offer humbly to your majesty."

"Tell your master," replied the King politely, "that I accept his present, and am very much obliged to him."

Another time Puss went and hid himself and his sack in a wheat-field, and there caught two splendid fat partridges in the same manner as he had done the rabbit. When he presented them to the King, with a similar message as before, His Majesty was so pleased that he ordered the cat to be taken down into the kitchen and given something to eat and drink; where, while enoying himself, the faithful animal talked in the most cunning way of the large preserves and abundant game which belonged to "my lord the Marquis of Carabas."

One day, hearing that the King was intending to take a drive along the riverside with his daughter, the most beautiful Princess in the world, Puss said to his master, "Sir, if you will only follow my advice, your fortune is made."

"Be it so," said the Miller's son, who was growing very disconsolate, and cared little what he did. "Say your say, cat."

"It is but little," replied Puss, looking wise, as cats can. "You have only to go and bathe in the river, at a place which I shall show you, and leave all the rest to me. Only remember that you are no longer yourself, but my lord the Marquis of Carabas."

"Just so," said the Miller's son, "it's all the same to me"; but he did as the cat told him.

While he was bathing, the King and all the Court passed by, and were startled to hear loud cries of "Help, help! My lord the Marquis of Carabas is drowning." The King put his head out of the carriage, and saw nobody but the cat, who had, at different times, brought him so many presents of game; however, he ordered his guards to fly quickly to the succour of my lord the Marquis of Carabas. While they were pulling the unfortunate Marquis out of the water, the cat came up, bowing, to the side of the King's carriage, and told a long and pitiful story about some thieves, who, while his master was bathing, had come and carried away all his clothes, so that it would be impossible for him to appear before His Majesty and the illustrious Princess.

"Oh, we will soon remedy that," answered the King kindly; and immediately ordered one of the first officers of the household to ride back to the palace with all speed, and bring back the most elegant supply of clothes for the young gentleman, who kept in the background until they arrived. Then, since he was handsome and well made, his new clothes became him so well that he looked as if he had been a marquis all his days, and advanced with an air of respectful ease to offer his thanks to His Majesty.

The King received him courteously, and the Princess admired him very much. Indeed, so charming did he appear to her that she hinted to her father to invite him into the carriage with them, which, you may be sure, the young man did not refuse. The cat, delighted at the success of his scheme, went away as fast as he could, and ran so swiftly that he kept a long way ahead of the royal carriage. He went on and on till he came to some peasants who were mowing in a meadow. "Good people," said he in a very firm voice, "the King is coming past here shortly; and if you do not say that the field you are mowing belongs to my lord the Marquis of Carabas, you shall all be chopped as small as mince-meat."

So when the King drove by, and asked whose meadow it was where there was such a splendid crop of hay, the mowers all answered, trembling, that it belonged to my lord the Marquis of Carabas.

"You have very fine land, Marquis," said His Majesty to the Miller's son, who bowed, and answered that it was not a bad meadow, take it altogether.

Then the cat came to a wheat-field, where the reapers were reaping with all their might. He bounced in upon them. "The King is coming past to-day, and if you do not tell him that this wheat belongs to my lord the Marquis of Carabas, I will have you every one chopped as small as

"Help, help! My lord the Marquis of Carabas is drowning."

22

"The King is coming past to-day."

mince-meat." The reapers, very much alarmed, did as they were bid, and the King congratulated the Marquis upon possessing such beautiful fields, laden with such an abundant harvest.

They drove on, the cat always running before and saying the same thing to everybody he met—that they were to declare the whole country belonged to his master; so that even the King was astonished at the vast estate of "my lord the Marquis of Carabas."

But now the cat arrived at a great castle where dwelt an Ogre, to whom belonged all the land through which the royal equipage had been driving. He was a cruel tyrant, and his tenants and servants were terribly afraid of him; which accounted for their being so ready to say whatever they were told to say by the cat, who had taken pains to inform himself all about the Ogre. So, putting on the boldest face he could assume, Puss marched up to the castle with his boots on, and asked to see the owner of it, saying that he was on his travels, but did not wish to pass so near the castle of such a noble gentleman without paying his respects to him. When the Ogre heard this message, he went to the door, received the cat as civilly as an Ogre can, and begged him to walk in and repose himself.

"Thank you, sir," said the cat, "but first I hope you will satisfy a traveller's curiosity. I have heard in far countries of your many remarkable qualities, and especially how you have the power of changing yourself into any sort of beast you choose—a lion, for instance, or an elephant."

"That is quite true," replied the Ogre; "and lest you should doubt it, I will immediately become a lion."

He did so; and the cat was so frightened that he sprang up to the roof of the castle and hid himself in the gutter—a proceeding rather inconvenient on account of his boots, which were not exactly fitted to walk with upon tiles. At length, perceiving that the Ogre had resumed his original form, he came down again stealthily, and confessed that he had been very much frightened.

"But, sir," said he, "it may be easy enough for such a big gentleman as you to change himself into a large animal; I do not suppose you can become a small one—a rat or a mouse, for instance. I have heard that you can; still, for my part, I consider it quite impossible."

"Impossible?" cried the other indignantly. "You shall see!" and immediately the cat saw the Ogre no longer, but a little mouse running along on the floor.

This was exactly what he wanted; and he did the very best a cat could do, and the most natural under the circumstances—he sprang upon the mouse and gobbled it up in a trice. So there was an end of the Ogre.

By this time the King had arrived opposite the castle, and was seized with a strong desire to enter it. The cat, hearing the noise of the carriage wheels, ran forward in a great hurry, and standing at the gate, said in a loud voice, "Welcome, Sire, to the castle of my lord the Marquis of Carabas."

"What!" cried His Majesty, very much surprised. "Does the castle also belong to you? Truly, Marquis, you have kept your secret well up to the last minute. I have never seen anything finer than this courtyard and these battlements. Indeed, I have nothing like them in the whole of my dominions."

The Marquis, without speaking, offered his hand to the Princess to assist her to descend, and standing aside that the King might enter first—for he had already acquired all the manners of a court—followed His Majesty to the great hall, where a magnificent collation was laid out, and where, without more delay, they all sat down to feast.

Before the banquet was over, the King, charmed with the good qualities of the Marquis of Carabas—and likewise with his wine, of which he had drunk six or seven cups—said, bowing across the table at which the Princess and the Miller's son were talking very confidentially together, "It rests with you, Marquis, whether you will not become my son-in-law."

"I shall be only too happy," said the complaisant Marquis, and the Princess's cast-down eyes declared the same.

So they were married the very next day, and took possession of the Ogre's castle, and of everything that had belonged to him.

As for the cat, he became at once a grand personage, and had nevermore any need to run *after mice, except for his own diversion.*

"I have heard in far countries of your many remarkable qualities."

29

The Strong Prince

Hungarian Folk Tale • Illustrated by H. J. Ford

Once upon a time there lived a King who was so fond of wine that he could not go to sleep unless he knew he had a great flaskful tied to his bed-post. All day long he drank till he was too stupid to attend to his business, and everything in the kingdom went to rack and ruin. But one day an accident happened to him, and he was struck on the head by a falling bough, so that he fell from his horse and lay dead upon the ground.

His wife and son mourned his loss bitterly, for in spite of his faults, he had always been kind to them. So they abandoned the crown and forsook their country, not knowing or caring where they went.

At length they wandered into a forest, and being very tired, sat down under a tree to eat some bread that they had brought with them. When they had finished, the Queen said, "My son, I am thirsty; fetch me some water."

The Prince got up at once and went to a brook which he heard gurgling near at hand. He stooped and filled his hat with the water, which he brought to his mother; then he turned and followed the stream up to its source in a rock, where it bubbled out clear and fresh and cold. He knelt down to take a draught from the deep pool below the rock when he saw the reflection of a sword hanging from the branch of a tree over his head. The young man drew back with a start; but in a moment he climbed the tree, cutting the rope which held the sword, and carried the weapon to his mother.

The Queen was greatly surprised at the sight of anything so splendid in such a lonely place, and took it in her hands to examine it closely. It was a curious workmanship, wrought with gold, and on its handle was written: "The man who can buckle on this sword will become stronger than other men." The Queen's heart swelled with joy as she read these words, and she bade her son lose no time in testing their truth. So he fastened it round his waist, and instantly a glow of strength seemed to run through his veins. He took hold of a thick oak tree and rooted it up as easily as if it had been a weed.

This discovery put new life into the Queen and her son, and they continued their walk through the forest. But night was drawing on, and the darkness grew so thick that it seemed as if it could be cut with a knife. They did not want to sleep in the wood, for they were afraid of wolves and other wild beasts, so they groped their way along, hand in hand, till the Prince tripped over something which lay across the path. He could not see what it was, but stooped down and tried to lift it. The thing was very heavy, and he thought his back would break under the strain. At last with a great heave he moved it out of the road, and as it fell he knew it was a huge rock. Behind the rock was a cave which it was quite clear was the home of some robbers, though not one of the band was there.

Hastily putting out the fire which burned brightly at the back, and bidding his mother come in and keep very still, the Prince began to pace up and down, listening for the return of the robbers. But he was very sleepy, and, in spite of all his efforts, he felt he could not keep awake much longer when he heard the sound of the robbers returning, shouting and singing as they marched along. Soon the singing ceased, and straining his ears, he heard them discussing anxiously what had become of their cave, and why they could not see the fire as usual. "This *must* be the place," said a voice, which the Prince took to be that of the Captain. "Yes, I feel the ditch before the entrance. Someone forgot to pile up the fire before we left and it has burnt itself out! But it is all right. Let every man jump across, and as he does so cry out 'Hop! I am here.' I will go last. Now begin."

The man who stood nearest jumped across, but he had no time to give the call which the Captain had ordered, for with one swift, silent stroke of the Prince's sword, his head rolled into the corner. Then the young man cried instead, "Hop! I am here."

The second man, hearing the signal, leapt the ditch in confidence, and was met by the same fate, and in a few minutes eleven of the robbers lay dead, and there remained only the Captain.

Now the Captain had wound round his neck the shawl of his lost wife, and the stroke of the Prince's sword fell harmless. Being very cunning, however, he made no resistance, and rolled over as if he were as dead as the other men. Still, the Prince was no fool, and wondered if indeed he was as dead as he seemed to be; but the Captain lay so stiff and stark that at last he was taken in.

The Prince next dragged the headless bodies into a chamber in the cave, and locked the door. Then he and his mother ransacked the place for some food, and when they had eaten it they lay down and slept in peace.

With the dawn they were both awake again, and found that, instead of the cave which they had come to the night before, they now were in a splendid castle, full of beautiful rooms. The Prince went round all these and carefully locked them up, bidding his mother take care of the keys while he was hunting.

Unfortunately, the Queen, like all women, could not bear to think that there was anything which she did not know. So the moment that her son had turned his back, she opened the doors of all the rooms, and peeped in, till she came to the one where the robbers lay. But if the sight of the blood on the ground turned her faint, the sight of the Robber Captain walking up and down was a greater shock still. She quickly turned the key in the lock, and ran back to the chamber she had slept in.

Soon after her son came in, bringing with him a large bear, which he had killed for supper. As there was enough food to last them for many days, the Prince did not hunt the next morning, but, instead, began to explore the castle. He found that a secret way led from it into the forest; and following the path, he reached another castle larger and more splendid than the one belonging to the robbers. He knocked at the door with his fist, and said that he wanted to enter; but the Giant, to whom the castle belonged, only answered: "I know who you are. I have nothing to do with robbers."

"I am no robber," answered the Prince. "I am the son of a King, and I have killed all the band. If you do not open to me at once I will break in the door, and your head shall go to join the others."

He waited a little, but the door remained shut as tightly as before. Then he just put his shoulder to it, and immediately the wood began to crack. When the Giant found that it was no use keeping it shut, he opened it, saying: "I see you are a brave youth. Let there be peace between us."

And the Prince was glad to make peace, for he had caught a glimpse of the Giant's beautiful daughter, and from that day he often sought the Giant's house.

Now the Queen led a dull life all alone in the castle, and to amuse herself she paid visits to the Robber Captain, who flattered her till at last she agreed to marry him. But as she was much afraid of her son, she told the Robber that the next time the Prince went to bathe in the river, he was to steal the sword from its place above the bed, for without it the young man would have no power to punish him for his boldness.

The Robber Captain thought this good counsel, and the next morning, when the young man went to bathe, he unhooked the sword from its nail and buckled it round his waist. On his return to the castle, the Prince found the Robber waiting for him on the steps, waving the sword above his head, and knowing that some horrible fate was in store, he fell on his knees and begged for mercy. But he might as well have tried to squeeze blood out of a stone. The Robber, indeed, granted him his life, but took out both his eyes, which he thrust into the prince's hand, saying brutally:

"Here you had better keep them! You may find them useful!"

Weeping, the blind youth felt his way to the Giant's house, and told him all the story.

The Giant was full of pity for the poor young man, but inquired anxiously what he had done with the eyes. The Prince drew them out of his pocket, and silently handed them to the Giant, who washed them well, and then put them back in the Prince's head. For three days he lay in utter darkness; then the light began to come back till soon he saw as well as ever.

But though he could not rejoice enough over the recovery of his eyes, he bewailed bitterly the loss of his sword, and that it should have fallen to the lot of his bitter enemy.

"Never mind, my friend," said the Giant, "I will get it back for you." And he sent for the monkey who was his head servant.

"Tell the fox and the squirrel that they are to go with you, and fetch me back the Prince's sword," ordered he.

The three servants set out at once, one seated on the back of the others, the ape, who disliked walking, being generally on top. Directly they came to the window of the Robber Captain's room, the monkey sprang from the backs of the fox and the squirrel, and climbed in. The room was empty, and the sword hanging from a nail. He took it down, and buckling it round his waist, as he had seen the Prince do, swung himself down again, and mounting on the backs of his two companions, hastened to his master. The Giant bade him give the sword to the Prince, who girded himself with it, and returned with all speed to the castle.

"Come out, you rascal! come out, you villain!" cried he, "and answer to me for the wrong you have done. I will show you who is the master in this house!"

The noise he made brought the Robber into the room. He glanced up to where the sword usually hung, but it was gone; and instinctively he looked at the Prince's hand, where he saw it gleaming brightly. In his turn he fell on his knees to beg for mercy, but it was too late. As he had done to the Prince, so the Prince did to him, and, blinded, he was thrust forth, and fell down a deep hole, where he is to this day. His mother the Prince sent back to her father, and never would see her again. After this he returned to the Giant, and said to him:

"My friend, add one more kindness to those you have already heaped on me. Give me your daughter as my wife."

So they were married, and the wedding feast was so splendid that there was not a kingdom in the world that did not hear of it. And the Prince never went back to his father's throne, but lived *peacefully with his wife in the forest, where, if they are not dead, they are living still.*

"I see you are a brave youth. Let there be peace between us."

32

The Strong Prince Enters the Giant's Castle. By H.J. Ford. 1903

They went every day to balls, plays, and public walks.

Beauty and the Beast

Jeanne Marie Leprince de Beaumont • Illustrated by Eleanor Vere Boyle

There was once a very rich Merchant who had six children, three boys and three girls. As he was himself a man of great sense, he spared no expense for their education. The three daughters were all handsome, but particularly the youngest—indeed she was so very beautiful that in her childhood every one called her the Little Beauty; and being equally lovely when she was grown up, nobody called her by any other name, which made her sisters very jealous of her. This youngest daughter was not only more handsome than her sisters, but was also better tempered. The two elder were vain of their wealth and position. They gave themselves a thousand airs, and refused to visit other merchants' daughters; nor would they condescend to be seen except with persons of quality. They went every day to balls, plays, and public walks, and always made game of their youngest sister for spending her time in reading or other useful employments. As it was well known that these young ladies would have large fortunes, many great merchants wished to get them for wives; but the two elder always answered that, for their part, they had no thoughts of marrying any one below a duke or an earl at least. Beauty had quite as many offers as her sisters, but she always answered, with the greatest civility, that though she was much obliged to her lovers, she would rather live some years longer with her father, as she thought herself too young to marry.

It happened that, by some unlucky accident, the Merchant suddenly lost all his fortune, and had nothing left but a small cottage in the country. Upon this he said to his daughters, while the tears ran down his cheeks, "My children, we must now go and dwell in the cottage, and try to get a living by labour, for we have no other means of support." The two elder replied that they did not know how to work, and would not leave town, for they had lovers enough who would be glad to marry them, though they had no longer any fortune. But in this they were mistaken, for when the lovers heard what had happened, they said, "The girls were so proud and ill tempered that all we wanted was their fortune. We are not sorry at all to see their pride brought down; let them show off their airs to their cows and sheep." But everybody pitied poor Beauty because she was so sweet-tempered and kind to all; and several gentlemen offered to marry her, though she had not a penny. But Beauty still refused, and said she could not think of leaving her poor father in this trouble. At first Beauty could not help sometimes crying in secret for the hardships she was now obliged to suffer; but in a very short time she said to herself, "All the crying in the world will do me no good, so I will try to be happy without a fortune."

When they had removed to their cottage, the Merchant and his three sons employed themselves in ploughing and sowing the fields and working in the garden. Beauty also did her part, for she rose by four o'clock every morning, lighted the fires, cleaned the house, and got ready the breakfast for the whole family. At first she found all this very hard, but she soon grew quite used to it, and thought it no hardship; indeed, the work greatly benefitted her health. When she had done, she used to amuse herself with reading, playing music, or singing while she spun. But her two sisters were at a loss what to do to pass the time away. They had their breakfast in bed, and did not rise till ten o'clock. Then they commonly walked out, but always found themselves very soon tired; when they would often sit down under a shady tree, and grieve for the loss of their carriage and fine clothes, and say to each other, "What a mean-spirited, poor, stupid creature our young sister is, to be so content with this low way of life!" But their father thought differently, and loved and admired his youngest child more than ever.

After they had lived in this manner about a year, the Merchant received a letter which informed him that one of his richest ships, which he thought was lost, had just come into port. This news made the two elder sisters almost mad with joy, for they thought they should now leave the cottage, and have all their finery again. When they found that their father must take a journey to the ship, the two elder begged he would not fail to bring them back some new gowns, caps, rings, and all sorts of trinkets. But Beauty asked for nothing, for she thought in herself that all the ship was worth would hardly buy everything her sisters wished for. "Beauty," said the Merchant, "how comes it that you ask for nothing? What can I bring you, my child?"

"Since you are so kind as to think of me, dear Father," she answered, "I should be glad if you would bring me a rose, for we have none in our garden." Now Beauty did not indeed wish for a rose, nor for anything else; she only said this that she might not affront her sisters; otherwise they would have said she wanted her father to praise her for desiring nothing.

The Merchant took his leave of them, and set out on his journey; but when he got to the ship some persons went to law with him about the cargo, and after a deal of trouble he had to go back to his cottage as poor as he had left it. When he was within thirty miles of his home, and thinking of the joy of again meeting his children, he lost his way in the midst of a dense forest. It rained very hard, and, besides, the wind was so high as to throw him twice from his horse.

Night came on, and he feared he should die of hunger, or be torn to pieces by the wolves that he heard howling round him. All at once he cast his eyes towards a long avenue, and saw at the end a light, but it seemed a great way off. He made the best of his way towards it, and found that it came from a splendid palace, the windows of which were all blazing with light. It had a gate, standing open, and fine courtyards beyond it, through which the Merchant passed; but not a living soul was to be seen. There were stables, too, which his poor starved horse, less scrupulous than himself, entered at once, and took a good meal of oats and hay. His master then tied him up, and walked towards the entrance hall, but still without seeing a single creature. He went on to a large dining-parlour, where he found a good fire, and a table covered with some very nice dishes, but only one plate with a knife and fork. As the rain had wetted him to the skin, he went up to the fire to dry himself. "I hope," said he, "the master of the house or his servants will excuse me, for it surely will not be long now before I see them."

He waited some time, but still nobody came. At last the clock struck eleven, and the Merchant, being quite faint for the want of food, helped himself to a chicken and to a few glasses of wine, yet all the time trembling with fear. He sat till the clock struck twelve, and then, taking courage, began to think he might as well look about him. So he opened a door at the end of the hall, and went through it into a very grand room, in which there was a fine bed; and as he was feeling very weary, he shut the door, took off his clothes, and got into it.

It was ten o'clock in the morning before he awoke, when he was amazed to see a handsome new suit of clothes laid ready for him instead of his own, which were all torn and spoiled. "To be sure," said he to himself, "this place belongs to some good Fairy who has taken pity on my ill luck."

It had a gate standing open.

36

Returning to the hall where he had supped, he found a breakfast table prepared. "Indeed, my good Fairy," said the Merchant aloud, "I am vastly obliged to you for your kind care of me." He then made a hearty breakfast, took his hat, and was going to the stable to pay his horse a visit; but as he passed under one of the arbours, which was loaded with roses, he thought of what Beauty had asked him to bring back to her, and so he took a bunch of roses to carry home. At the same moment he heard a loud noise, and saw coming towards him a Beast, so frightful to look at that he was ready to faint with fear. "Ungrateful man!" said the Beast in a terrible voice. "I have saved your life by admitting you into my palace, and in return you steal my roses, which I value more than anything I possess. But you shall atone for your fault: you shall die in a quarter of an hour."

The Merchant fell on his knees, and clasping his hands, said, "Sir, I humbly beg your pardon. I did not think it would offend you to gather a rose for one of my daughters, who had entreated me to bring her one home. Do not kill me, my lord!"

"I am not a Lord, but a Beast," replied the monster. "I hate false compliments, so do not fancy that you can coax me by any such ways. You tell me that you have daughters; now I will suffer you to escape if one of them will come and die in your stead. If not, promise that you will yourself return in three months, to be dealt with as I may choose."

The tender-hearted Merchant had no thoughts of letting any one of his daughters die for his sake; but he knew that if he seemed to accept the Beast's terms, he should at least have the pleasure of seeing them once again. So he gave his promise, and was told he might then set off as soon as he liked. "But," said the Beast, "I do not wish you to go back empty-handed. Go to the room you slept in, and you will find a chest there; fill it with whatsoever you like best, and I will have it taken to your own house for you."

When the Beast had said this, he went away. The good Merchant, left to himself, began to consider that as he must die—for he had no thought of breaking a promise made even to a Beast—he might as well have the comfort of leaving his children provided for. He returned to the room he had slept in, and found there heaps of gold pieces lying about. He filled the chest with them to the very brim, locked it, and, mounting his horse, left the palace as sorrowful as he had been glad when he first beheld it. The horse took a path across the forest of his own accord, and in a few hours they reached the Merchant's house. His children came running round him, but instead of kissing them with joy, he could not help weeping as he looked at them. He held in his hand the bunch of roses, which he gave to Beauty, saying, "Take these roses, Beauty, but little do you know how dear they have cost your poor father"; and then he gave them an account of all that he had seen or heard in the palace of the Beast.

The two elder sisters now began to shed tears, and to lay the blame upon Beauty, who, they said, would be the cause of their father's death. "See," said they, "what happens from the pride of the little wretch; why did not she ask for such things as we did? But, to be sure, Miss must not be like other people; and though she will be the cause of her father's death, yet she does not shed a tear."

"It would be useless," replied Beauty, "for my father shall not die. As the Beast will accept of one of his daughters, I will give myself up, and be only too happy to prove my love for the best of fathers."

"No, sister," said the three brothers with one voice, "that cannot be; we will go in search of this Monster, and either he or we will perish."

"Do not hope to kill him," said the Merchant; "his power is far too great. But Beauty's young life shall not be sacrificed. I am old, and cannot expect to live much longer; so I shall but give up a few years of my life, and shall only grieve for the sake of my children."

"Never, Father!" cried Beauty. "If you go back to the palace, you cannot hinder my going after you. Though young, I am not over-fond of life; and I would much rather be eaten up by the Monster than die of grief for your loss."

The Merchant in vain tried to reason with Beauty, who still obstinately kept to her purpose, which, in truth, made her two sisters glad, for they were jealous of her because everybody loved her.

The Merchant was so grieved at the thought of losing his child that he never once thought of the chest filled with gold; but at night, to his great surprise, he found it standing by his bedside. He said nothing about his riches to his elder daughters, for he knew very well it would at once make them want to return to town; but he told Beauty his secret, and she then said 'that while he was away two gentlemen had been on a visit to their cottage, who had fallen in love with her two sisters. She entreated her father to marry them without delay, for she was so sweet-natured she only wished them to be happy.

Three months went by, only too fast, and then the Merchant and Beauty got ready to set out for the palace of the Beast. Upon this, the two sisters rubbed their eyes with an onion to make believe they were crying; both the Merchant and his sons cried in earnest. Only Beauty shed no tears. They reached the palace in a very few hours, and the horse, without bidding, went into the same stable as before. The Merchant and Beauty walked towards the large hall, where they found a table covered with every dainty, and two plates laid ready. The Merchant had very little appetite, but Beauty, that she might the better hide her grief, placed herself at the table, and helped her father; she then began to eat herself, and thought all the time that to be sure the Beast had a mind to fatten her before he ate her up, since he had provided such good cheer for her. When they had taken their supper, they heard a great noise, and the good old man began to bid his poor child farewell, for he knew it was the Beast coming to them. When Beauty first saw that frightful form, she was very much terrified, but tried to hide her fear. The creature walked up to her and eyed her all over, then asked her in a dreadful voice if she had come quite of her own accord.

"Yes," said Beauty.

"Then you are a good girl, and I am much obliged to you."

This was such an astonishingly civil answer that Beauty's courage rose; but it sank again when the Beast, addressing the Merchant, desired him to leave the palace next morning and never return to it again. "And so good-night, Merchant. . . . And good-night, Beauty."

"Good-night, Beast," she answered as the Monster shuffled out of the room.

"Ah, my dear child!" said the Merchant, kissing his daughter. "I am half dead already at the thought of leaving you with this dreadful Beast; you shall go back and let me stay in your place."

"No," said Beauty boldly, "I will never agree to that; you must go home to-morrow morning."

They then wished each other good-night and went to bed, both of them thinking they should not be able to close their eyes; but as soon as ever they had lain down they fell into a deep sleep, and did not awake till morning. Beauty dreamed that a Lady came up to her, who said, "I am very much pleased, Beauty, with the goodness you have shown in being willing to give your life to save that of your father. Do not be afraid of anything; you shall not go without a reward."

As soon as Beauty awoke she told her father this dream; but though it gave him some comfort, it was a long time before he could be persuaded to leave the palace. At last Beauty succeeded in getting him safely away.

When her father was out of sight, poor Beauty began to weep sorely; still, having naturally a courageous spirit, she soon resolved not to make her sad case still worse by sorrow, which she knew was vain, but to wait and be patient. She walked about to take a view of all the palace, and the elegance of every part of it much charmed her.

But what was her surprise when she came to a door on which was written, BEAUTY'S ROOM! She opened it in haste, and her eyes were dazzled by the splendour and taste of the apartment. What made her wonder more than all the rest were a large library filled with books, a harpsichord, and many pieces of music. "The Beast surely does not mean to eat me up immediately," said she, "since he takes care I shall not be at a loss how to amuse myself." She opened the library, and saw these verses written in letters of gold on the back of one of the books:

Beauteous lady, dry your tears,
Here's no cause for sighs or fears,
Command as freely as you may,
For you command and I obey.

"Alas!" said she, sighing. "I wish I could only command a sight of my poor father, and to know what he is doing at this moment." Just then, by chance, she cast her eyes on a looking-glass that stood near her, and in it she saw a picture of her old home, and her father riding mournfully up to the door. Her sisters came out to meet him, and although they tried to look sorry, it was easy to see that in their hearts they were very glad. In a short time all this picture disappeared, but it caused Beauty to think that the Beast, besides being very powerful, was also very kind. About the middle of the day she found a table laid ready for her, and a sweet concert of music played all the time she was dining, without her seeing anybody. But at supper, when she was seating herself at table, she heard the noise of the Beast, and could not help trembling with fear.

"Beauty," said he, "will you give me leave to see you sup?"

"That is as you please," answered she, very much afraid.

"Not in the least," said the Beast; "you alone command in this place. If you should not like my company, you need only say so, and I will leave you that moment. But tell me, Beauty, do you not think me very ugly?"

"Why, yes," said she, "for I cannot tell a falsehood; but then I think you are very good."

"Am I?" sadly replied the Beast. "Yet, besides being ugly, I am also very stupid: I know well enough that I am but a beast."

"Very stupid people," said Beauty, "are never aware of it themselves."

At which kindly speech the Beast looked pleased, and replied, not without an awkward sort of politeness, "Pray do not let me detain you from supper, and be sure that you are well served. All you see is your own, and I should be deeply grieved if you wanted for anything."

"You are very kind—so kind that I almost forgot you are so ugly," said Beauty earnestly.

"Ah yes!" answered the Beast with a great sigh. "I hope I am good-tempered, but still I am only a monster."

"There is many a monster who wears the form of a man; it is better of the two to have the heart of a man and the form of a monster."

"I would thank you, Beauty, for this speech, but I am too senseless to say anything that would please you," returned the Beast in a melancholy voice; and altogether he seemed so gentle and so unhappy that Beauty, who had the tenderest heart in the world, felt her fear of him gradually vanish.

She ate her supper with a good appetite, and conversed in her own sensible and charming way, till at last, when the Beast was ready to depart, he terrified her more than ever by saying abruptly, in his gruff voice, "Beauty, will you marry me?"

He terrified her more than ever by saying abruptly,
in his gruff voice, "Beauty, will you marry me?"

Now Beauty, frightened as she was, would speak only the exact truth; besides, her father had told her that the Beast liked to have only the truth spoken to him. So she answered, in a very firm tone, "No, Beast."

He did not go into a passion, or do anything but sigh deeply and depart.

When Beauty found herself alone, she began to feel pity for the poor Beast. "Oh," said she, "what a sad thing it is that he should be so very frightful, since he is so good-tempered!"

Beauty lived three months in this palace very well pleased. The Beast came to see her every night, and talked with her while she supped; and though what he said was not very clever, yet, as she saw in him every day some new goodness, instead of dreading the time of his coming, she soon began continually looking at her watch, to see if it was nine o'clock, for that was the hour when he never failed to visit her. Only one thing vexed her, which was that every night, before he went away, he always made it a rule to ask her if she would be his wife, and seemed very much grieved at her steadfastly replying "No." At last, one night, she said to him, "You wound me greatly, Beast, by forcing me to refuse you so often. I wish I could take such a liking to you as to agree to marry you, but I must tell you plainly that I do not think it will ever happen. I shall always be your friend, so try to let that content you."

"I must," sighed the Beast, "for I know well enough how frightful I am; but I love you better than myself. Yet I think I am very lucky in your being pleased to stay with me. Now promise me, Beauty, that you will never leave me."

Beauty would almost have agreed to this, so sorry was she for him; but she had that day seen in her magic glass, which she looked at constantly, that her father was dying of grief for her sake.

"Alas!" she said. "I long so much to see my father that, if you do not give me leave to visit him, I shall break my heart."

"I would rather break mine, Beauty," answered the Beast. "I will send you to your father's cottage; you shall stay there, and your poor Beast shall die of sorrow."

"No," said Beauty, crying, "I love you too well to be the cause of your death; I promise to return in a week. You have shown me that my sisters are married, and my brothers are gone to be soldiers, so that my father is left all alone. Let me stay a week with him."

"You shall find yourself with him to-morrow morning," replied the Beast, "but mind, do not forget your promise. When you wish to return, you have nothing to do but to put your ring on a table when you go to bed. Good-bye, Beauty!" The Beast sighed as he said these words, and Beauty went to bed very sorry to see him so much grieved. When she awoke in the morning, she found herself in her father's cottage. She rang a bell that was at her bedside, and a servant entered, but as soon as she saw Beauty, the woman gave a loud shriek; upon which the Merchant ran upstairs, and when he beheld his daughter he ran to her, and kissed her a hundred times. At last Beauty began to remember that she had brought no clothes with her to put on; but the servant told her she had just found in the next room a large chest full of dresses, trimmed all over with gold, and adorned with pearls and diamonds.

Beauty, in her own mind, thanked the Beast for his kindness, and put on the plainest gown she could find among them all. She then desired the servant to lay the rest aside, for she intended to give them to her sisters; but as soon as she had spoken these words the chest was gone out of sight. Her father then suggested that perhaps the Beast chose that she should keep them all for herself; and as soon as he had said this, they saw the chest standing again in the same place. While Beauty was dressing herself, a servant brought word to her that her sisters were come with their husbands to pay her a visit. They both lived unhappily with the gentlemen they had married. The husband of the eldest was very handsome, but was so proud of this that he thought of nothing else from morning till night, and did not care a pin for the beauty of his wife. The second had married a man of great learning, but he made no use of it, except to torment and affront all his friends, and his wife more than any of them. The two sisters were ready to burst with spite when they saw Beauty dressed like a Princess and looking so very charming. All the kindness that she showed them was of no use, for they were vexed more than ever when she told them how happily she lived at the palace of the Beast. The spiteful creatures went by themselves into the garden, where they cried to think of her good fortune.

"Why should the little wretch be better off than we?" said they. "We are much handsomer than she is."

"Sister," said the eldest, "a thought has just come into my head: let us try to keep her here longer than the week for which the Beast gave her leave, and then he will be so angry that perhaps when she goes back to him he will eat her up in a moment."

"That is well thought of," answered the other, "but to do this we must pretend to be very kind."

They then went to join her in the cottage, where they showed her so much false love that Beauty could not help crying for joy.

When the week was ended, the two sisters began to pretend such grief at the thought of her leaving them that she agreed to stay a week more; but all that time Beauty could not help fretting for the sorrow that she knew her absence would give her poor Beast, for she tenderly loved him, and much wished for his company again. Among all the grand and clever people she saw, she found nobody who was half so sensible, so affectionate, so thoughtful, or so kind. The tenth night of her being at the cottage she dreamed she was in the garden of the palace, that the Beast lay dying on a grass plot, and with his last breath put her in mind of her promise, and laid his death to her forsaking him. Beauty awoke in a great fright, and burst into tears. "Am not I wicked," said she, "to behave so ill to a Beast who has shown me so much kindness? Why will not I marry him? I am sure I should be more happy with him than my sisters are with their husbands. He shall not be wretched any longer on my account, for I should do nothing but blame myself all the rest of my life."

She then rose, put her ring on the table, got into bed again, and soon fell asleep. In the morning she with joy found herself in the palace of the Beast. She dressed herself very carefully that she might please him the better, and thought she had never known a day pass away so slowly. At last the clock struck nine, but the Beast did not come. Beauty, dreading lest she might truly have caused his death, ran from room to room, calling out, "Beast, dear Beast"; but there was no answer. At last she remembered her dream, rushed to the grass plot, and there saw him lying, apparently dead, beside the fountain. Forgetting all his ugliness, she threw herself upon his body; and finding his heart still beat, she fetched some water and sprinkled it over him, weeping and sobbing the while.

The Beast opened his eyes. "You forgot your promise, Beauty, and so I determined to die; for I could not live without you. I have starved myself to death, but I shall die content, since I have seen your face once more."

"No, dear Beast," cried Beauty passionately, "you shall not die; you shall live to be my husband. I thought it was only friendship I felt for you, but now I know it was love."

The moment Beauty had spoken these words the palace was suddenly lighted up, and all kinds of rejoicings were heard around them, none of which she noticed, but hung over her dear Beast with the utmost tenderness. At last, unable to restrain herself, she dropped her head over her hands, covered her eyes, and cried for joy; and, when she looked up again, the Beast was gone. In his stead she saw at her feet a handsome, graceful young Prince, who thanked her with the tenderest expressions for having freed him from enchantment.

"But where is my poor Beast? I only want him and nobody else," sobbed Beauty.

"I am he," replied the Prince. "A wicked Fairy condemned me to this form, and forbade me to show that I had any wit or sense till a beautiful lady should consent to marry me. You alone, dearest Beauty, judged me neither by my looks nor by my talents, but by my heart alone. Take it then, and all that I have besides, for all is yours."

Beauty, full of surprise, but very happy, suffered the Prince to lead her into his palace, where she soon found her father and sisters, who had been brought there by the Fairy Lady whom she had seen in a dream the first night she came.

"Beauty," said the Fairy, "you have chosen well, and you have your reward, for a true heart is better than either good looks or clever brains. . . . As for you, ladies," and she turned to the two elder sisters, "I know all your ill deeds, but I have no worse punishment for you than to see your sister happy. You shall stand as statues at the door of her palace, and when you repent of and have amended your faults, you shall become women again. But, to tell you the truth, I *very much fear you will remain statues for ever.*"

Beauty, full of surprise, but very happy, suffered the Prince to lead her into his palace.

Rumpelstiltskin

Jacob and Wilhelm Grimm • Illustrated by George Cruikshank

There was once a Miller who was very poor, but he had a beautiful daughter. Now, it happened that he came to speak to the King, and to give himself importance, he said to him, "I have a daughter who can spin straw into gold."

The King said to the Miller, "That is a talent that pleases me well; if she be as skilful as you say, bring her to-morrow to the palace, and I will put her to the proof."

When the Maiden was brought to him, he led her to a room full of straw, gave her a wheel and spindle, and said, "Now set to work, and if by the morrow this straw be not spun into gold, you shall die." He locked the door, and left the Maiden alone.

The poor Girl sat down disconsolate, and could not for her life think what she was to do, for she knew not—how could she?—the way to spin straw into gold; and her distress increased so much that at last she began to weep. All at once the door opened, and a little man entered and said, "Good-evening, my pretty Miller's daughter; why are you weeping so bitterly?"

"Ah!" answered the Maiden. "I must spin straw into gold, and know not how to do it."

The little man said, "What will you give me if I do it for you?"

"My neckerchief," said the Maiden.

He took the kerchief, sat down before the wheel, and grind, grind, grind—three times did he grind—and the spindle was full; then he put another thread on, and grind, grind, grind—the second was full; so he spun on till morning, when all the straw was spun, and all the spindles were full of gold."

The King came at sunrise, and was greatly astonished and overjoyed at the sight; but it only made his heart the more greedy of gold. He put the Miller's daughter into another much larger room, full of straw, and ordered her to spin it all in one night, if life were dear to her. The poor helpless Maiden began to weep, when once more the door flew open, and the little man appeared, and said, "What will you give me if I spin this straw into gold?"

"My ring from my finger," answered the Maiden.

The little man took the ring, began to turn the wheel, and by the morning all the straw was spun into shining gold.

The King was highly delighted when he saw it, but was not yet satisfied with the quantity of gold; so he put the Damsel into a still larger room full of straw, and said, "Spin this during the night; and if you do it you shall be my wife." For, he thought, if she's only a Miller's daughter, I shall never find a richer wife in the whole world.

As soon as the Damsel was alone, the little man came the third time and said, "What will you give me if I again spin all this straw for you?"

"I have nothing more to give you," answered the Girl.

"Then promise, if you become Queen, to give me your first child."

Who knows how that may be, or how things may turn out between now and then? thought

46

the Girl, but in her perplexity she could not help herself; so she promised the little man what he desired, and he spun all the straw into gold.

When the King came in the morning and saw that his orders had been obeyed, he married the Maiden, and the beautiful Miller's daughter became a Queen. After a year had passed she brought a lovely baby into the world, but quite forgot the little man till he walked suddenly into her chamber, and said, "Give me what you promised me." The Queen was frightened, and offered him all the riches of the kingdom if he would only leave her the child, but he answered, "No; something living is dearer to me than all the treasures of the world."

Then the Queen began to grieve and to weep so bitterly that the little man took pity upon her and said, "I will give you three days; if in that time you can find out my name, you shall keep the child."

All night long the Queen thought over every name she had ever heard, and sent a messenger through the kingdom to inquire what names were usually given to people in that country. When, next day, the little man came again, she began with Casper, Melchior, Balthazar, and repeated, each after each, all the names she knew or had heard of; but at each one the little man said, "That is not my name."

The second day she again sent round about in all directions, to ask how the people were called, and repeated to the little man the strangest names she could hear of or imagine. To each he answered always, "That is not my name."

The third day the messenger returned and said, "I have not been able to find a single new name; but as I came over a high mountain by a wood, where the fox and the hare bid each other good-night, I saw a little house, and before the house was burning a little fire, and round the fire danced a very funny little man, who hopped upon one leg, and cried out:

'To-day I brew, to-morrow I bake,
Next day the Queen's child I shall take,
How glad I am that nobody knows
My name is Rumpelstiltskin!' "

You may guess how joyful the Queen was at hearing this; and when, soon after, the little man entered and said, "Queen, what is my name?" she asked him mischievously, "Is your name Kunz?"

"No."

"Is your name Carl?"

"No."

"Are you not sometimes called Rumpelstiltskin?"

"A Witch has told you that—a Witch has told you!" shrieked the poor little man, and stamped so furiously with his right foot that it sunk into the floor; then with both hands he *seized his left foot with such violence that he tore himself right in two.*

The Princess and the Peas

Hans Christian Andersen • Illustrated by Edmund Dulac

There lived, once upon a time, a Prince, and he wished to marry a Princess, but then she must be really and truly a Princess. So he travelled over the whole world to find one, but there was always something or other to prevent his being successful. Princesses he found in plenty, but he never could make out if they were real Princesses, for sometimes one thing and sometimes another appeared to him not quite right about the ladies. So at last he returned home quite cast down; for he wanted so very much to have a real Princess for a wife.

One evening a dreadful storm was gathering; it thundered and lightened, and the rain poured down from heaven in torrents; it was, too, as dark as pitch. Suddenly a loud knocking was heard at the town-gates, and the old King, the Prince's father, went out himself to see who was there.

It was a Princess that stood at the gate, but, Lord bless me, what a figure she was from the rain! The water ran down from her hair, and her dress was dripping wet and stuck quite close to her body. She said she was a real Princess.

We'll soon see that, thought the old Queen Dowager; however, she said not a word, but went into the bed-room, took out all the bedding, and laid three small peas on the bottom of the bed-stead. Then she took, first, twenty mattresses, and laid them one upon the other on the three peas, and then she took twenty feather-beds more, and put these again a-top of the mattresses.

This was the bed the Princess was to sleep in.

The next morning she asked her if she had had a good night.

"Oh no, a horrid night!" said the Princess. "I was hardly able to close my eyes the whole night! Heaven knows what was in my bed, but there was a something hard under me, and my whole body is black and blue with bruises! I can't tell you what I've suffered!"

Then they knew that the lady they had lodged was a real Princess, since she had felt the three small peas through twenty mattresses and twenty feather-beds; for it was quite impossible for any one but a true Princess to be so tender.

So the Prince married her, for he was now convinced that he had a real Princess for his wife. The three peas were deposited in the Museum, where they are still to be seen; that is to say, if they have not been lost.

Now was not that a lady of exquisite feeling?

49

"I can't tell you what I've suffered."

Bearskin

Written and Illustrated by Howard Pyle

There was a King travelling through the country, and he and those with him were so far away from home that darkness caught them by the heels, and they had to stop at a stone mill for the night because there was no other place handy.

While they sat at supper they heard a sound in the next room, and it was a baby crying.

The Miller stood in the corner, back of the stove, with his hat in his hand. "What is that noise?" said the King to him.

"Oh! It is nothing but another baby that the good storks have brought into the house to-day," said the Miller.

Now there was a wise man travelling along with the King who could read the stars and everything that they told as easily as one can read one's ABCs in a book after one knows them, and the King, for a bit of jest, would have him find out what the stars had to foretell of the Miller's baby. So the wise man went out and took a peep up in the sky, and by and by he came in again.

"Well," said the King, "and what did the stars tell you?"

"The stars tell me," said the wise man, "that you shall have a daughter, and that the Miller's baby, in the room yonder, shall marry her when they are old enough to think of such things."

"What!" said the King. "And is a miller's baby to marry the Princess that is to come! We will see about that." So the next day he took the Miller aside and talked and bargained, and bargained and talked, until the upshot of the matter was that the Miller was paid two hundred dollars, and the King rode off with the baby.

As soon as he came home to the castle, he called his chief forester to him. "Here," says he, "take this baby and do thus and so with it, and when you have killed it bring its heart to me, that I may know that you have really done as you have been told."

So off marched the forester with the baby; but on his way he stopped at home, and there was his good wife working about the house.

"Well, Henry," said she, "what do you do with the baby?"

"Oh!" said he. "I am just taking it off to the forest to do thus and so with it."

"Come," said she, "it would be a pity to harm the little innocent, and to have its blood on your hands. Yonder hangs the rabbit that you shot this morning, and its heart will please the King just as well as the other."

Thus the wife talked, and the end of the business was that she and the man smeared a basket all over with pitch and set the baby adrift in it on the river, and the King was just as well satisfied with the rabbit's heart as he would have been with the baby's.

But the basket with the baby in it drifted on and on down the river until it lodged at last

50

It lodged at last among the high reeds that stood along the bank.

among the high reeds that stood along the bank. By and by there came a great She-Bear to the water to drink, and there she found it.

Now the huntsmen in the forest had robbed the She-Bear of her cubs, so that her heart yearned over the little baby, and she carried it home with her to fill the place of her own young ones. There the baby throve until he grew to a great strong lad, and as he fed upon nothing but bear's milk for all that time, he was ten times stronger than the strongest man in the land.

One day, as he was walking through the forest, he came across a woodman chopping the trees into billets of wood, and that was the first time he had ever seen a body like himself. Back he went to the Bear as fast as he could travel, and told her what he had seen. "That," said the Bear, "is the most wicked and most cruel of all the beasts."

"Yes," says the lad, "that may be so; all the same I love beasts like that as I love the food I eat, and I long for nothing so much as to go out into the wide world, where I may find others of the same kind."

At this the Bear saw very well how the geese flew and that the lad would soon be flitting.

"See," said she, "if you must go out into the wide world, you must. But you will be wanting help before long, for the ways of the world are not peaceful and simple as they are here in the woods, and before you have lived there long, you will have more needs than there are flies in summer. See, here is a little crooked horn, and when your wants grow many, just come to the forest and blow a blast on it, and I will not be too far away to help you."

So off went the lad away from the forest, and all the coat he had upon his back was the skin of a bear dressed with the hair on it, and that was why folk called him "Bearskin."

He trudged along the high-road until he came to the King's castle, and it was the same King who thought he had put Bearskin safe out of the way years and years ago.

Now the King's Swineherd was in want of a lad, and as there was nothing better to do in that town, Bearskin took the place and went every morning to help drive the pigs into the forest, where they might eat the acorns and grow fat.

One day there was a mighty stir throughout the town, folk crying and making a great hubbub. "What is it all about?" says Bearskin to the Swineherd.

What! And did he not know what the trouble was? Where had he been for all of his life that he had heard nothing of what was going on in the world? Had he never heard of the great fiery Dragon with three heads that had threatened to lay waste all of that land unless the pretty Princess was given up to him? This was the very day that the Dragon was to come for her, and she was to be sent up on the hill back of the town; that was why all the folk were crying and making such a stir.

"So!" says Bearskin. "And is there never a lad in the whole country that is man enough to face the beast? Then I will go myself if nobody better is to be found." And off he went, though the Swineherd laughed and laughed, and thought it all a bit of a jest. By and by Bearskin came to the forest, and there he blew a blast upon the little crooked horn that the Bear had given him.

Presently came the Bear through the bushes, so fast that the little twigs flew behind her. "And what is it that you want?" said she.

"I should like," said Bearskin, "to have a horse, a suit of gold-and-silver armour that nothing can pierce, and a sword that shall cut through iron and steel, for I would like to go up on the hill to fight the Dragon and free the pretty Princess at the King's town over yonder."

"Very well," said the Bear, "look back of the tree yonder, and you will find just what you want."

Yes; sure enough, there they were back of the tree: a grand white horse that champed his bit and pawed the ground till the gravel flew, and a suit of gold-and-silver armour such as a king

The Princess gave him what he asked for, and a sweet kiss into the bargain (page 53).

might wear. Bearskin put on the armour and mounted the horse, and off he rode to the high hill back of the town.

By and by came the Princess and the Steward of the castle, for it was he that was to bring her to the Dragon. But the Steward stayed at the bottom of the hill, for he was afraid, and the Princess had to climb it alone, though she could hardly see the road before her for the tears that fell from her eyes. But when she reached the top of the hill, she found instead of the Dragon a fine tall fellow dressed all in gold-and-silver armour. And it did not take Bearskin long to comfort the Princess, I can tell you. "Come, come," says he, "dry your eyes and cry no more; all the cakes in the oven are not burnt yet; just go back of the bushes yonder, and leave it with me to talk the matter over with Master Dragon."

The Princess was glad enough to do that. Back of the bushes she went, and Bearskin waited for the Dragon to come. He had not long to wait either, for presently it came flying through the air, so that the wind rattled under his wings.

Dear, dear! If one could but have been there to see that fight between Bearskin and the Dragon, for it was well worth the seeing, and that you may believe. The Dragon spit out flames and smoke like a house afire. But he could do no hurt to Bearskin, for the gold-and-silver armour sheltered him so well that not so much as one single hair of his head was singed. So Bearskin just rattled away the blows at the Dragon—slish, slash, snip, clip—until all three heads were off, and there was an end of it.

After that he cut out the tongues from the three heads of the Dragon, and tied them up in his pocket-handkerchief.

Then the Princess came out from behind the bushes, where she had lain hidden, and begged Bearskin to go back with her to the King's castle, for the King had said that if any one killed the Dragon, he should have her for his wife. But no; Bearskin would not go to the castle just now, for the time was not yet ripe; but, if the Princess would give them to him, he would like to have the ring from her finger, the kerchief from her bosom, and the necklace of golden beads from her neck.

The Princess gave him what he asked for, and a sweet kiss into the bargain, and then Bearskin mounted upon his grand white horse and rode away to the forest. "Here are your horse and armour," said he to the Bear, "and they have done good service to-day, I can tell you." Then he tramped back again to the King's castle with the old bear's skin over his shoulders.

"Well," says the Swineherd, "and did you kill the Dragon?"

"Oh yes," says Bearskin, "I did that, but it was no such great thing to do after all."

At that the Swineherd laughed and laughed, for he did not believe a word of it.

And now listen to what happened to the Princess after Bearskin had left her. The Steward came sneaking up to see how matters had turned out, and there he found her safe and sound, and the Dragon dead. "Whoever did this left luck behind him," said he, and he drew his sword and told the Princess that he would kill her if she did not swear to say nothing of what had happened. Then he gathered up the Dragon's three heads, and he and the Princess went back to the castle.

"There!" said he when they had come before the King, and he flung down the three heads upon the floor. "I have killed the Dragon, and I have brought back the Princess, and now if anything is to be had for the labour, I would like to have it." As for the Princess, she wept and wept, but she could say nothing, and so it was fixed that she was to marry the Steward, for that was what the King had promised.

At last came the wedding-day, and the smoke went up from the chimneys in clouds, for there was to be a grand wedding-feast, and there was no end of good things cooking for those who were to come.

As for the Princess, she wept and wept, but she could say nothing.

"See now," says Bearskin to the Swineherd where they were feeding their pigs together, out in the woods, "as I killed the Dragon over yonder, I ought at least to have some of the good things from the King's kitchen; you shall go and ask for some of the fine white bread and meat, such as the King and Princess are to eat to-day."

Dear, dear, but you should have seen how the Swineherd stared at this and how he laughed, for he thought the other must have gone out of his wits; but as for going to the castle—no, he would not go a step, and that was the long and the short of it.

"So! Well, we will see about that," says Bearskin, and he stepped to a thicket and cut a good stout stick, and without another word caught the Swineherd by the collar, and began dusting his jacket for him until it smoked again.

"Stop, stop!" bawled the Swineherd.

"Very well," says Bearskin; "and now will you go over to the castle for me, and ask for some of the same bread and meat that the King and Princess are to have for their dinner?"

Yes, yes; the Swineherd would do anything that Bearskin wanted.

"So! Good!" says Bearskin. "Then just take this ring and see that the Princess gets it; and say that the lad who sent it would like to have some of the bread and meat that she is to have for her dinner."

So the Swineherd took the ring, and off he started to do as he had been told. Rap! Tap! Tap! he knocked at the door. Well, and what did he want?

Oh! There was a lad over in the woods yonder who had sent him to ask for some of the same bread and meat that the King and Princess were to have for their dinner, and he had brought this ring to the Princess as a token.

But how the Princess opened her eyes when she saw the ring which she had given to Bearskin upon the hill! For she saw, as plain as the nose on her face, that he who had saved her from the Dragon was not so far away as she had thought. Down she went into the kitchen herself to see that the very best bread and meat were sent, and the Swineherd marched off happily with a great basket full of it.

"Yes," says Bearskin, "that is very well so far, but I am for having some of the red and white wine that they are to drink. Just take this kerchief over to the castle yonder, and let the Princess know that the lad to whom she gave it upon the hill back of the town would like to have a taste of the wine that she and the King are to have at the feast to-day."

Well, the Swineherd was for saying "no" to this as he had to the other, but Bearskin just reached his hand over towards the stout stick that he had used before, and the other started off as though the ground were hot under his feet. And what was the Swineherd wanting this time—that was what they said over at the castle.

"The lad with the pigs in the woods yonder," says the Swineherd, "must have gone crazy, for he has sent this kerchief to the Princess and says that he should like to have a bottle or two of the wine that she and the King are to drink to-day."

When the Princess saw her kerchief, again her heart leapt for joy. She made no two words about the wine, but went down into the cellar and brought it up with her own hands, and the Swineherd marched off with it tucked under his coat.

"Yes, that was all very well," said Bearskin; "I am satisfied so far as the wine is concerned, but now I would like to have some of the sweetmeats that they are to eat at the castle to-day. See, here is a necklace of golden beads; just take it to the Princess and ask for some of those sweetmeats, for I will have them," and this time he had only to look towards the stick, and the other started off as fast as he could travel.

The Swineherd had no more trouble with this asking than with the others, for the Princess went down-stairs and brought the sweetmeats from the pantry with her own hands, and the Swineherd carried them to Bearskin where he sat out in the woods with the pigs.

Then Bearskin spread out the good things, and he and the Swineherd sat down to the feast together, and a fine one it was, I can tell you.

"And now," says Bearskin when they had eaten all that they could, "it is time for me to leave you, for I must go and marry the Princess." So off he started, and the Swineherd did nothing but stand and gape after him, with his mouth open, as though he were set to catch flies. But Bearskin went straight to the woods, and there he blew upon his horn, and the Bear was with him as quickly this time as the last.

"Well, what do you want now?" said she.

"This time," said Bearskin, "I want a fine suit of clothes made of gold-and-silver cloth, and a horse to ride on up to the King's house, for I am going to marry the Princess."

Very well; there was what he wanted back of the tree yonder; and it was a suit of clothes fit for a great King to wear, and a splendid dapple grey horse with a golden saddle and bridle studded all over with precious stones. So Bearskin put on the clothes and rode away, and a fine sight he was to see, I can tell you.

And how the folks stared when he rode up to the King's castle. Out came the King along with the rest, for he thought that Bearskin was some great lord. But the Princess knew him the moment she set eyes upon him, for she was not likely to forget him so soon as all that.

The King brought Bearskin into where they were feasting, and had a place set for him alongside of himself.

The Steward was there along with the rest. "See," said Bearskin to him, "I have a question to put. One killed a Dragon and saved a Princess, but another came and swore falsely that he did it. Now, what should be done to such a one?"

"Why, this," said the Steward, speaking up as bold as brass, for he thought to face the matter down, "he should be put in a cask stuck all round with nails, and dragged behind three wild horses."

"Very well," said Bearskin, "you have spoken for yourself. For I killed the Dragon up on the hill behind the town, and you stole the glory of the doing."

"That is not so," said the Steward, "for it was I who brought home the three heads of the Dragon in my own hand, and how can that be with the rest?"

Then Bearskin stepped to the wall where hung the three heads of the Dragon. He opened the mouth of each. "And where are the tongues?" said he.

At this the Steward grew as pale as death; nevertheless, he still spoke up as boldly as ever. "Dragons have no tongues," said he. But Bearskin only laughed; he untied his handkerchief before them all, and there were the three tongues. He put one in each mouth, and they fitted exactly, and after that no one could doubt that he was the hero who had really killed the Dragon. So when the wedding came, it was Bearskin, and not the Steward, who married the Princess; what was done to him you may guess for yourselves.

And so had a grand wedding, but in the very midst of the feast one came running in and said there was a great brown bear without who would come in, will-nilly. Yes, and you have guessed it right, it *was* the great She-Bear, and if nobody else was made much of at that wedding, you can depend upon it that she was.

As for the King, he was satisfied that the Princess had married a great hero. So she had, only he was the Miller's son after all, though the King knew no more of that than my grandfather's little dog, and no more did anybody but the wise man for the matter of that, and he said nothing of it, *for wise folk don't tell all they know.*

The Sleeping Beauty in the Wood

Charles Perrault • Illustrated by Walter Crane

Once there was a royal couple who grieved excessively because they had no children. When at last, after long waiting, the Queen presented her husband with a little daughter, His Majesty showed his joy by giving a christening feast so grand that the like of it was never known. He invited all the Fairies in the land—there were seven altogether—to stand Godmothers to the little Princess, hoping that each might bestow on her some good gift, as was the custom of good Fairies in those days.

After the ceremony all the guests returned to the palace, where there was set before each Fairy Godmother a magnificent covered dish, with an embroidered table-napkin, and a knife and work of pure gold, studded with diamonds and rubies. But, alas! As they placed themselves at table, there entered an old Fairy who had never been invited, because more than fifty years since she had left the King's dominion on a tour of pleasure, and had not been heard of until this day. His Majesty, much troubled, desired a cover to be placed for her; but it was of common delf, for he had ordered from his jeweller only seven gold dishes for the seven Fairies aforesaid. The elderly Fairy thought herself neglected, and muttered angry menaces, which were overheard by one of the younger Fairies who chanced to sit beside her. This good Godmother, afraid of harm to the pretty baby, hastened to hide herself behind the tapestry in the hall. She did this because she wished all the others to speak first, so that, if any ill gift were bestowed on the child, she might be able to counteract it.

The six now offered their good wishes—which, unlike most wishes, were sure to come true. The fortunate little Princess was to grow up the fairest woman in the world, to have a temper sweet as an angel, to be perfectly graceful and gracious, to sing like a nightingale, to dance like a leaf on a tree, and to possess every accomplishment under the sun. Then the old Fairy's turn came. Shaking her head spitefully, she uttered the wish that when the baby grew up into a young lady, and learned to spin, she might prick her finger with the spindle and die of the wound.

At this terrible prophecy all the guests shuddered, and some of the more tender-hearted began to weep. The lately happy parents were almost out of their wits with grief. Upon which the wise young Fairy appeared from behind the tapestry, saying cheerfully, "Your Majesties may comfort yourselves: the Princess shall not die. I have no power to alter the ill-fortune just wished her by my ancient sister—her finger must be pierced; and she shall then sink, not into the sleep of death, but into a sleep that will last a hundred years. After that time is ended, the son of a King will find her, awaken her, and marry her."

Immediately all the Fairies vanished.

The King, in the hope of preventing his daughter's doom, issued an edict forbidding all persons to spin, and even to have spinning-wheels in their houses, on pain of instant death. But it was in vain. One day, when she was just fifteen years of age, the King and Queen left their daughter alone in one of their castles, when, wandering about at her will, she came to an ancient donjon tower, climbed to the top of it, and there found a very old woman—so old and deaf that she had never heard of the King's edict—busy with her wheel.

"What are you doing, good old woman?" said the Princess.

"I'm spinning, my pretty child."

"Ah, how charming! Let me try if I can spin also."

She had no sooner taken up the spindle than, being lively and obstinate, she handled it so awkwardly and carelessly that the point pierced her finger. Though it was so small a wound, she fainted away at once, and dropped silently down on the floor. The poor frightened old woman called for help; shortly came the ladies-in-waiting, who tried every means to restore their young mistress, but all their care was useless. She lay, beautiful as an angel, the colour still lingering in her lips and cheeks; her fair bosom softly stirred with her breath, but her eyes were fast closed. When the King, her father, and the Queen, her mother, beheld her thus, they knew regret was idle—all had happened as the cruel Fairy meant. But they also knew that their daughter would not sleep for ever, though after one hundred years it was not likely that either of them would behold her awakening. Until that happy hour should arrive, they determined to leave her in repose. They sent away all the physicians and attendants, and themselves sorrowfully laid her upon a bed of embroidery, in the most elegant apartment of the palace. There she slept, and looked like a sleeping angel still.

When this misfortune happened, the kindly young Fairy who had saved the Princess by changing her sleep of death into this sleep of a hundred years was twelve thousand leagues away in the kingdom of Mataquin. But being informed of everything, she arrived speedily in a chariot of fire drawn by Dragons. The King was somewhat startled by the sight, but nevertheless went to the door of his palace, and, with a mournful countenance, presented her his hand to descend.

The Fairy condoled with His Majesty, and approved of all he had done. Then, being a Fairy of great common sense and foresight, she suggested that the Princess, awakening after a hundred years in this ancient castle, might be a good deal embarrassed, especially with a young Prince by her side, to find herself alone. Accordingly, without asking any one's leave, she touched with her magic wand the entire population of the palace, except the King and Queen; governesses, ladies of honour, waiting-maids, gentlemen ushers, cooks, kitchen-girls, pages, footmen—down to the horses that were in the stables, and the grooms that attended them—she touched each and all. Nay, with kind consideration for the feelings of the Princess, she even touched the little fat lapdog, Puffy, who had laid himself down beside his mistress on her splendid bed. He, like all the rest, fell fast asleep in a moment. The very spits that were before the kitchen fire ceased turning, and the fire itself went out, and everything became as silent as if it were the middle of the night, or as if the palace were a palace of the dead.

The King and Queen—having kissed their daughter and wept over her a little, but not much, she looked so sweet and content—departed from the castle, giving orders that it was to be approached no more. The command was unnecessary: in one quarter of an hour there sprang up around it a wood so thick and thorny that neither beasts nor men could attempt to penetrate there. Above this dense mass of forest could be perceived only the top of the high tower where the lovely Princess slept.

A great many changes happen in a hundred years. The King, who never had a second child, died, and his throne passed to another royal family. So entirely was the story of the poor Princess forgotten that when the reigning King's son, being one day out hunting and stopped in the chase by this formidable wood, inquired what wood it was and what were those towers which he saw appearing out of the midst of it, no one could answer him. At length an old peasant was found who remembered having heard his grandfather say to his father that in this tower was a Princess, beautiful as the day, who was doomed to sleep there for one hundred years, until awakened by a King's son, her destined bridegroom.

At this the young Prince, who had the spirit of a hero, determined to find out the truth for himself. Spurred on by both generosity and curiosity, he leapt from his horse and began to force his way through the thick wood. To his amazement the stiff branches all gave way, and the ugly thorns sheathed themselves of their own accord, and the brambles buried themselves in the earth to let him pass. This done, they closed behind him, allowing none of his suite to follow; but, ardent and young, he went boldly on alone.

The first thing he saw was enough to smite him with fear. Bodies of men and horses lay extended on the ground; but the men had faces, not death-white, but red as peonies, and beside them were glasses half filled with wine, showing that they had gone to sleep drinking. Next he entered a large court, paved with marble, where stood rows of guards presenting arms, but motionless as if cut out of stone; then he passed through many chambers where gentlemen and ladies, all in the costume of the past century, slept at their ease, some standing, some sitting. The pages were lurking in corners, the ladies of honour were stooping over their embroidery frames, or listening, apparently with polite attention, to the gentlemen of the court; but all were as silent as statues and as immovable. Their clothes, strange to say, were fresh and new as ever; and not a particle of dust or spider-web had gathered over the furniture, though it had not known a broom for a hundred years. Finally the astonished Prince came to an inner chamber where was the fairest sight his eyes had ever beheld.

A young girl of wonderful beauty lay asleep on an embroidered bed, and she looked as if she had only just closed her eyes. Trembling, the Prince approached and knelt beside her. Some say he kissed her; but as nobody saw it, and she never told, we cannot be quite sure of that. However, as the end of the enchantment had come, the Princess awakened at once, and looking at him with eyes of the tenderest regard, said drowsily, "Is it you, my Prince? I have waited for you very long."

Charmed with these words, and still more with the tone in which they were uttered, the Prince assured her that he loved her more than his life. Nevertheless, he was the more embarrassed of the two, for, thanks to the kind Fairy, the Princess had plenty of time to dream of him during her century of slumber, while he had never even heard of her till an hour before. For a long time did they sit conversing, and yet had not said half enough. Their only interruption came from the little dog Puffy, who had awakened with his mistress, and now began to be exceedingly jealous that the Princess did not notice him as much as she was wont to do.

Meantime all the attendants, whose enchantment was also broken, not being in love, were ready to die of hunger after their fast of a hundred years. A lady of honour ventured to intimate

60

Trembling, the Prince approached and knelt beside her.

that dinner was served; whereupon the Prince handed his beloved Princess at once to the great hall. She did not wait to dress for dinner, being already perfectly and magnificently attired, though in a fashion somewhat out of date. However, her lover had the politeness not to notice this, nor to remind her that she was dressed exactly like her royal grandmother, whose portrait still hung on the palace walls.

During the banquet a concert took place by the attendant musicians, and considering that they had not touched their instruments for a century, they played extremely well. They ended with a wedding march, for that very evening the marriage of the Prince and Princess was celebrated, and though the bride was nearly one hundred years older than the bridegroom, it is remarkable that the fact would never have been discovered by any one unacquainted therewith.

After a few days they went together out of the castle and the enchanted wood, both of which immediately vanished, and were never more beheld by mortal eyes. The Princess was restored to her ancestral kingdom; but it was not generally declared who she was, as during a hundred years people had grown so very much wiser that nobody then living would ever have believed the story. So nothing was explained, and nobody presumed to ask any questions about her, for ought not a Prince to be free to marry whomsoever he pleases?

Nor—whether or not the day of Fairies was over—did the Princess ever see anything further of her seven Godmothers. She lived a long and happy life, like any other ordinary woman, and *died at length, beloved, regretted, but, the Prince being already no more, perfectly contented.*

The Frog Prince

Jacob and Wilhelm Grimm • Illustrated by Walter Crane

In times of yore, when wishes were both heard and granted, lived a King whose daughters were all beautiful; but the youngest was so lovely that the sun himself, who has seen so much, wondered at her beauty every time he looked in her face. Now near the King's castle was a large dark forest; and in the forest, under an old linden tree, was a deep well. When the day was very hot, the King's daughter used to go to the wood and seat herself at the edge of the cool well; and when she became wearied, she would take a golden ball, throw it up in the air, and catch it again. This was her favourite amusement. Once it happened that her golden ball, instead of falling back into the little hand that she stretched out for it, dropped on the ground, and immediately rolled away into the water. The King's daughter followed it with her eyes; but the ball had vanished, and the well was so deep that no one could see down to the bottom. Then she began to weep, wept louder and louder every minute, and could not console herself at all.

While she was thus lamenting, some one called to her: "What is the matter with you, King's daughter? You weep so that you would touch the heart of a stone."

She looked around to see whence the voice came, and saw a Frog stretching his thick ugly head out of the water.

"Ah, it is you, old water-paddler!" said she. "I am crying for my golden ball, which has fallen into the well."

"Be content," answered the Frog. "I daresay I can give you some good advice; but what will you give me if I bring back your plaything to you?"

"Whatever you like, dear Frog," said she "—my clothes, my pearls, and jewels, even the golden crown I wear."

The Frog answered, "Your clothes, your pearls and jewels, even your golden crown, I do not care for; but if you will love me, and let me be your companion and playfellow, sit near you at your little table, eat from your little golden plate, drink from your little cup, and sleep in your little bed—if you will promise me this—then I will bring you back your golden ball from the bottom of the well."

"Oh yes!" said she. "I promise you everything if you will only bring me back my golden ball."

She thought to herself meanwhile: What nonsense the silly Frog talks! He sits on the water with the other frogs, and croaks, and cannot be anybody's playfellow!

But the Frog, as soon as he had received the promise, dipped his head under the water and sank down. In a little while up he came again with the ball in his mouth, and threw it on the

63

grass. The King's daughter was overjoyed when she beheld her pretty plaything again, picked it up, and ran away with it.

"Wait! Wait!" cried the Frog. "Take me with you. I cannot run as fast as you."

Alas! Of what use was it that he croaked after her as loud as he could? She would not listen to him, but hastened home, and soon forgot the poor Frog, who was obliged to plunge again to the bottom of his well.

The next day, when she was sitting at dinner with the King and all the courtiers, eating from her little gold plate, there came a sound of something creeping up the marble staircase—splish, splash—and when it had reached the top, it knocked at the door and cried, "Youngest King's daughter, open to me."

She ran, wishing to see who was outside; but when she opened the door, and there sat the Frog, she flung it hastily to again, and sat down at table, feeling very, very uncomfortable. The King saw that her heart was beating violently, and said, "How, my child, why are you afraid? Is a Giant standing outside the door to carry you off?"

"Oh no!" answered she, "it is no Giant, but a nasty Frog, who yesterday, when I was playing in the wood near the well, fetched my golden ball out of the water. For this I promised him he should be my companion, but I never thought he could come out of his well. Now he is at the door, and wants to come in."

Again, the second time, there was a knock, and a voice cried:

"Youngest King's daughter,
    Open to me;
Know you what yesterday
    You promised me,
By the cool water?
Youngest King's daughter,
    Open to me."

Then said the King, "What you promised you must perform. Go and open the door."

She went and opened the door; the Frog hopped in, always following and following her till he came up to her chair. There he sat, and cried out, "Lift me up to you on the table."

She refused till the King, her father, commanded her to do it. When the Frog was on the table, he said, "Now push your little golden plate nearer to me, that we may eat together." She did as he desired, but one could easily see that she did it unwillingly. The Frog seemed to enjoy his dinner very much, but every morsel she ate stuck in the throat of the poor little Princess.

Then said the Frog, "I have eaten enough, and am tired; carry me to your little room, and make your little silken bed smooth, and we will lay ourselves down to sleep together."

At this the daughter of the King began to weep, for she was afraid of the cold Frog, who wanted to sleep in her pretty clean bed.

But the King looked angrily at her, and said again, "What you have promised you must perform. The Frog is your companion."

It was no use to complain: whether she liked it or not, she was obliged to take the Frog with her up to her little bed. So she picked him up with two fingers, hating him bitterly the while, and carried him upstairs; but when she got into bed, instead of lifting him up to her, she threw him with all her strength against the wall, saying, "Now, you nasty Frog, there will be an end of you."

She did as he desired, but one could easily see that she did it unwillingly.

But what fell down from the wall was not a dead Frog, but a living young Prince, with beautiful and loving eyes, who at once became, by her own promise and her father's will, her dear companion and husband. He told her how he had been cursed by a wicked sorceress, and that no one but the King's youngest daughter could release him from his enchantment and take him out of the well.

The next day a carriage drove up to the palace gates with eight white horses, having white feathers on their heads and golden reins. Behind it stood the servant of the young Prince, called the Faithful Henry. This Faithful Henry had been so grieved when his master was changed into a Frog that he had been compelled to have three iron bands fastened round his heart, lest it should break. Now the carriage came to convey the Prince to his kingdom, so the Faithful Henry lifted in the bride and bridegroom, and mounted behind, full of joy at his lord's release. But when they had gone a short distance, the Prince heard behind him a noise as if something were breaking. He turned round, and cried out, "Henry, the carriage is breaking!"

But Henry replied, "No, sir, it is not the carriage, but one of the bands from my heart, with which I was forced to bind it up or it would have broken with grief, while you sat as a Frog at the bottom of the well."

Twice again this happened, and the Prince always thought the carriage was breaking, but it was only the bands breaking off from the heart of the Faithful Henry, out of joy that his lord the *Frog Prince was a Frog no more.*

Snowdrop

Jacob and Wilhelm Grimm • Illustrated by Arthur Rackham

It was the middle of winter, and the snowflakes were falling from the sky like feathers. Now a Queen sat sewing at a window framed in black ebony, and as she sewed she looked out upon the snow. Suddenly she pricked her finger and three drops of blood fell on to the snow. And the red looked so lovely on the white that she thought to herself: If only I had a child as white as snow and as red as blood, and as black as the wood of the window frame! Soon after, she had a daughter, whose hair was black as ebony, while her cheeks were red as blood, and her skin as white as snow, so she was called Snowdrop. But when the child was born, the Queen died. A year after, the King took another wife. She was a handsome woman, but proud and overbearing, and she could not endure that anyone should surpass her in beauty. She had a miraculous looking-glass, and when she stood before it and looked at herself, she used to say:

> "Mirror, Mirror on the wall,
> Who is fairest of us all?"

Then the Glass answered:

> "Queen, thou'rt fairest of them all."

Then she was content, for she knew that the looking-glass spoke the truth.

But Snowdrop grew up and became more and more beautiful, so that when she was seven years old, she was as beautiful as the day, and far surpassed the Queen. Once, when she asked her Glass:

> "Mirror, Mirror on the wall,
> Who is fairest of us all?"

It answered:

> "Queen, thee fairest here I hold,
> But Snowdrop fairer thousandfold."

Then the Queen was horror-struck, and turned green and yellow with jealousy. From the hour that she saw Snowdrop her heart sank, and she hated the little girl.

The pride and envy of her heart grew like a weed, so that she had no rest day nor night. At last she called a Huntsman, and said: "Take the child out into the wood; I will not set eyes to her again; you must kill her and bring me her lungs and liver as tokens."

69

The Huntsman obeyed, and took Snowdrop out into the forest, but when he drew his hunting knife and was preparing to plunge it into her innocent heart, she began to cry.

"Alas! Dear Huntsman, spare my life, and I will run away into the wild forest and never come back again."

And because of her beauty the Huntsman had pity on her and said, "Well, run away, poor child." Wild beasts will soon devour you, he thought, but still he felt as though a weight were lifted from his heart because he had not been obliged to kill her. And as just at that moment a young fawn came leaping by, he pierced it and took the lungs and liver as tokens to the Queen. The Cook was ordered to serve them up in pickle, and the wicked Queen ate them thinking that they were Snowdrop's.

Now the poor child was alone in the great wood, with no living soul near, and she was so frightened that she glanced at all the leaves on the trees and knew not what to do. Then she began to run, and ran over the sharp stones and through the brambles, while the animals passed her by without harming her. She ran as far as her feet could carry her till it was nearly evening; then she saw a little house and went in to rest. Inside, everything was small, but as neat and clean as could be. A small table covered with a white cloth stood ready with seven small plates, and by every plate was a spoon, knife, fork, and cup. Seven little beds were ranged against the walls, covered with snow-white coverlets. As Snowdrop was very hungry and thirsty, she ate a little bread and vegetable from each plate and drank a little wine from each cup, for she did not want to eat up the whole of one portion. Then, being very tired, she lay down in a bed, but none suited her; one was too short, another too long, all except the seventh, which was just right. She remained in it, said her prayers, and fell asleep.

When it was quite dark, the masters of the house came in. They were seven Dwarfs, who used to dig in the mountains for ore. They kindled their lights, and as soon as they could see, they noticed that someone had been there, for everything was not in the order in which they had left it.

The first said, "Who has been sitting in my chair?"

The second said, "Who has been eating off my plate?"

The third said, "Who has been nibbling my bread?"

The fourth said, "Who has been eating my vegetables?"

The fifth said, "Who has been using my fork?"

The sixth said, "Who has been cutting with my knife?"

The seventh said, "Who has been drinking out of my cup?"

Then the first looked and saw a slight impression on his bed, and said, "Who has been treading on my bed?" The others came running up and said, "And mine, and mine?" But the seventh, when he looked into his bed, saw Snowdrop, who lay there asleep. He called the others, who came up and cried out with astonishment as they held their lights and gazed at Snowdrop. "Heavens! What a beautiful child," they said, and they were so delighted that they did not wake her up but left her asleep in bed. But the seventh Dwarf slept with his comrades, an hour with each all through the night.

When morning came, Snowdrop woke up, and when she saw the seven Dwarfs, she was frightened.

But they were very kind and asked her name.

"I am called Snowdrop," she answered.

"How did you get into our house?" they asked.

Then she told them how her stepmother had wished to get rid of her, how the Huntsman had spared her life, and how she had run all day till she had found the house.

Then the Dwarfs said, "Will you look after our household, cook, make the beds, wash, sew

When they saw she was laced too tight, they cut the lace, whereupon she began to breathe and soon came back to life again (page 72).

and knit, and keep everything neat and clean? Then you shall stay with us and want for nothing."

"Yes," said Snowdrop, "with all my heart"; and she stayed with them and kept the house in order.

In the morning they went to the mountain and searched for copper and gold, and in the evening they came back and then their meal had to be ready. All day the maiden was alone, and the good Dwarfs warned her and said, "Beware of your stepmother, who will soon learn that you are here. Don't let anyone in."

But the Queen, having, as she imagined, eaten Snowdrop's liver and lungs, and feeling certain that she was the fairest of all, stepped in front of her Glass, and asked:

"Mirror, Mirror on the wall,
Who is fairest of us all?"

The Glass answered as usual:

"Queen, thee fairest here I hold,
But Snowdrop over the fells,
Who with the seven Dwarfs dwells,
Fairer still a thousandfold."

She was dismayed, for she knew that the Glass told no lies, and she saw that the Hunter had deceived her and that Snowdrop still lived. Accordingly she began to wonder afresh how she might compass her death, for as long as she was not the fairest in the land, her jealous heart left her no rest. At last she thought of a plan. She dyed her face and dressed up like an old Pedlar, so that she was quite unrecognizable. In this guise she crossed over the seven mountains to the home of the seven Dwarfs and called out, "Wares for sale."

Snowdrop peeped out of the window and said, "Good-day, mother, what have you got to sell?"

"Good wares, fine wares," she answered, "laces of every colour," and she held out one which was made of gay plaited silk.

I may let the honest woman in, thought Snowdrop, and she unbolted the door and bought the pretty lace.

"Child," said the Old Woman, "what a sight you are, I will lace you properly for once."

Snowdrop made no objection, and placed herself before the Old Woman to let her lace her with the new lace. But the Old Woman laced so quickly and tightly that she took away Snowdrop's breath, and she fell down as though dead.

"Now I am the fairest," she said to herself, and hurried away.

Not long after the seven Dwarfs came home and were horror-struck when they saw their dear little Snowdrop lying on the floor without stirring, like one dead. When they saw she was laced too tight, they cut the lace, whereupon she began to breathe and soon came back to life again. When the Dwarfs heard what had happened, they said that the old Pedlar was no other than the wicked Queen. "Take care not to let anyone in when we are not here," they said.

Now the wicked Queen, as soon as she got home, went to the Glass and asked:

"Mirror, Mirror on the wall,
Who is fairest of us all?"

And it answered as usual:

> "Queen, thee fairest here I hold,
> But Snowdrop over the fells,
> Who with the seven Dwarfs dwells,
> Fairer still a thousandfold."

When she heard it, all her blood flew to her heart, so enraged was she, for she knew that Snowdrop had come back to life again. Then she thought to herself, I must plan something which will put an end to her. By means of witchcraft, in which she was skilled, she made a poisoned comb. Next she disguised herself and took the form of a different Old Woman. She crossed the mountains and came to the home of the seven Dwarfs and knocked at the door, calling out, "Good wares to sell."

Snowdrop looked out of the window and said, "Go away, I must not let any one in."

"At least you may look," answered the Old Woman, and she took the poisoned comb and held it up.

The child was so pleased with it that she let herself be beguiled, and opened the door.

When she had made a bargain, the Old Woman said, "Now I will comb your hair properly for once."

Poor Snowdrop, suspecting no evil, let the Old Woman have her way, but scarcely was the poisoned comb fixed in her hair than the poison took effect, and the maiden fell down unconscious.

"You paragon of beauty," said the sinful woman, "now it is all over with you," and she went away.

Happily it was near the time when the seven Dwarfs came home. When they saw Snowdrop lying on the ground as though dead, they immediately suspected her stepmother, and searched till they found the poisoned comb. No sooner had they removed it than Snowdrop came to herself again and related what had happened. They warned her again to be on her guard, and to open the door to no one.

When she got home, the Queen stood before her Glass and said:

> "Mirror, Mirror on the wall,
> Who is fairest of us all?"

And it answered as usual:

> "Queen, thee fairest here I hold,
> But Snowdrop over the fells,
> Who with the seven Dwarfs dwells,
> Fairer still a thousandfold."

When she heard the Glass speak these words, she trembled and quivered with rage. "Snowdrop shall die," she said, "even if it cost me my own life." Thereupon she went into a secret room, which no one ever entered but herself, and made a poisonous apple. Outwardly it was beautiful to look upon, pale, with rosy cheeks, and everyone who saw it longed for it, but whoever ate of it was certain to die. When the apple was ready, she dyed her face and dressed herself like an old Peasant Woman and so crossed the seven hills to the Dwarfs' home. There she knocked.

Snowdrop put her head out of the window and said, "I must not let anyone in, the seven Dwarfs have forbidden me."

"It is all the same to me," said the Peasant Woman. "I shall soon get rid of my apples. There,

73

I will give you one."

"No, I must not take anything."

"Are you afraid of poison?" said the woman. "See, I will cut the apple in half: you eat the red side and I will keep the pale."

Now the apple was so cunningly painted that the red half alone was poisoned. Snowdrop longed for the apple, and when she saw the Peasant Woman eating, she could hold out no longer; she stretched out her hand and took the poisoned half. Scarcely had she put a bit into her mouth than she fell dead to the ground.

The Queen looked with a fiendish glance, and laughed aloud and said, "White as snow, red as blood, and black as ebony, this time the Dwarfs cannot wake you up again." And when she got home and asked the Looking-Glass:

"Mirror, Mirror on the wall,
Who is fairest of us all?"

It answered at last:

"Queen, thou'rt fairest of them all."

Then her jealous heart was at rest, as much at rest as a jealous heart can be. The Dwarfs, when they came at evening, found Snowdrop lying on the ground, and not a breath escaped her lips, and she was quite dead. They lifted her up and looked to see whether any poison was to be found, unlaced her dress, combed her hair, washed her with wine and water, but it was no use: their dear child was dead. They laid her on a bier, and all seven sat down and bewailed her and lamented over her for three whole days. Then they prepared to bury her, but she looked so fresh and living, and still had such beautiful rosy cheeks, that they said, "We cannot sink her in the dark earth." And so they had a transparent glass coffin made so that she could be seen from every side, laid her inside, and wrote on it in letters of gold her name and how she was a King's daughter. Then they set the coffin out on the mountain, and one of them always stayed by and watched it. And the birds came too and bewailed Snowdrop, first an owl, then a raven, and lastly a dove.

Now Snowdrop lay a long, long time in her coffin, looking as though she were asleep. It happened that a Prince was wandering in the wood, and came to the home of the seven Dwarfs to pass the night. He saw the coffin on the mountain and lovely Snowdrop inside, and read what was written in golden letters. Then he said to the Dwarfs, "Let me have the coffin; I will give you whatever you like for it."

But they said, "We will not give it up for all the gold of the world."

Then he said, "Then give it to me as a gift, for I cannot live without Snowdrop to gaze upon, and I will honour and reverence it as my dearest treasure."

When he had said these words, the good Dwarfs pitied him and gave him the coffin.

The Prince bade his servants carry it on their shoulders. Now it happened that they stumbled over some brushwood, and the shock dislodged the piece of apple from Snowdrop's throat. In a short time she opened her eyes, lifted the lid of the coffin, sat up, and came back to life again completely.

"Heavens! Where am I?" she asked.

The Prince, full of joy, said, "You are with me," and he related what had happened, and then said, "I love you better than all the world; come with me to my father's castle and be my wife."

Snowdrop agreed and went with him, and their wedding was celebrated with great magnificence. Snowdrop's wicked stepmother was invited to the feast, and when she had put on her fine clothes, she stepped to her Glass and asked:

"Mirror, Mirror on the wall,
Who is fairest of us all?"

The Glass answered:

"Queen, thee fairest here I hold,
The young Queen fairer thousandfold."

Then the wicked woman uttered a curse, and was so terribly frightened that she didn't know what to do. Yet she had no rest; she felt obliged to go and see the young Queen. And when she came in, she recognized Snowdrop, and stood stock still with fear and terror. But iron slippers were heated over the fire, and were soon brought in with tongs and put before her. And she had *to step into the red-hot shoes and dance till she fell down dead.*

The Water of Life

Jacob and Wilhelm Grimm • Illustrated by Arthur Rackham

There was once a King who was so ill that it was thought impossible his life could be saved. He had three sons, and they were all in great distress on his account, and they went into the castle gardens and wept at the thought that he must die. An old man came up to them and asked the cause of their grief. They told him that their father was dying, and nothing could save him. The old man said, "There is only one remedy which I know; it is the Water of Life. If he drinks of it, he will recover, but it is very difficult to find."

The eldest son said, "I will soon find it"; and he went to the sick man to ask permission to go in search of the Water of Life, as that was the only thing to cure him.

"No," said the King. "The danger is too great. I would rather die."

But he persisted so long that at last the King gave his permission.

The Prince thought, If I bring this water, I shall be the favourite, and I shall inherit the kingdom.

So he set off, and when he had ridden some distance he came upon a Dwarf standing on the road who cried, "Whither away so fast?"

"Stupid little fellow," said the Prince, proudly; "what business is it of yours?" and rode on.

The little man was very angry, and made an evil vow.

Soon after, the Prince came to a gorge in the mountains, and the farther he rode the narrower it became, till he could go no farther. His horse could neither go forward nor turn round for him to dismount; so there he sat, jammed in.

The sick King waited a long time for him, but he never came back. Then the second son said, "Father, let me go and find the Water of Life," thinking, If my brother is dead, I shall have the kingdom.

The King at first refused to let him go, but at last he gave his consent. So the Prince started on the same road as his brother, and met the same Dwarf, who stopped him and asked where he was going in such a hurry.

"Little Snippet, what does it matter to you?" he said, and rode away without looking back.

But the Dwarf cast a spell over him, and he, too, got into a narrow gorge like his brother, where he could go neither backwards nor forwards.

This is what happens to the haughty.

As the second son also stayed away, the youngest one offered to go and fetch the Water of Life, and at last the King was obliged to let him go.

When he met the Dwarf, and he asked him where he was hurrying to, he stopped and said, "I am searching for the Water of Life, because my father is dying."

"Do you know where it is to be found?"

"No," said the Prince.

76

"As you have spoken pleasantly to me, and not been haughty like your false brothers, I will help you and tell you how to find the Water of Life. It flows from a fountain in the courtyard of an enchanted castle, but you will never get in unless I give you an iron rod and two loaves of bread. With the rod strike three times on the iron gate of the castle, and it will spring open. Inside you will find two Lions with wide-open jaws, but if you throw a loaf to each, they will be quiet. Then you must make haste to fetch the Water of Life before it strikes twelve, or the gates of the castle will close and you will be shut in."

The Prince thanked him, took the rod and the loaves, and set off. When he reached the castle, all was just as the Dwarf had said. At the third knock the gate flew open, and when he had pacified the Lions with the loaves, he walked into the castle. In the great hall he found several enchanted Princes, and he took the rings from their fingers. He also took a sword and a loaf which were lying by them. On passing into the next room, he found a beautiful Maiden, who rejoiced at his coming. She embraced him, and said that he had saved her, and should have the whole of her kingdom; and if he would come back in a year, she would marry him. She also told him where to find the fountain with the enchanted water; but, she said, he must make haste to get out of the castle before the clock struck twelve.

Then he went on, and came to a room where there was a beautiful bed freshly made, and as he was very tired he thought he would take a little rest; so he lay down and fell asleep. When he woke, it was striking a quarter to twelve. He sprang up in a fright, and ran to the fountain, and took some of the water in a cup which was lying near, and then hurried away. The clock struck just as he reached the iron gate, and it banged so quickly that it took off a bit of his heel.

He was rejoiced at having got some of the Water of Life, and hastened on his homeward journey. He again passed the Dwarf, who, when he saw the sword and the loaf, said, "Those things will be of much service to you. You will be able to strike down whole armies with the sword, and the loaf will never come to an end."

The Prince did not want to go home without his brothers, and he said, "Good Dwarf, can you not tell me where my brothers are? They went in search of the Water of Life before I did, but they never came back."

"They are both stuck fast in a narrow mountain gorge. I cast a spell over them because of their pride."

Then the Prince begged so hard that they might be released that at last the Dwarf yielded; but he warned him against them, and said, "Beware of them; they have bad hearts."

He was delighted to see his brothers when they came back, and told them all that had happened to him: how he had found the Water of Life, and brought a goblet full with him. How he had released a beautiful Princess, who would wait a year for him and then marry him, and he would become a great Prince.

Then they rode away together, and came to a land where famine and war were raging. The King thought he would be utterly ruined, so great was the destitution.

The Prince went to him and gave him the loaf, and with it he fed and satisfied his whole kingdom. The Prince also gave him his sword, and he smote the whole army of his enemies with it, and then he was able to live in peace and quiet. Then the Prince took back his sword and his loaf, and the three brothers rode on. But they had to pass through two more countries where war and famine were raging, and each time the Prince gave his sword and his loaf to the King, and in this way he saved three kingdoms.

After that they took a ship and crossed the sea. During the passage the two elder brothers said to each other, "Our youngest brother found the Water of Life, and we did not, so our father will give him the kingdom, which we ought to have, and he will take away the luck from us."

77

This thought made them very vindictive, and they made up their minds to get rid of him. They waited till he was asleep, and then they emptied the Water of Life from his goblet and took it themselves, and filled up his cup with salt sea-water.

As soon as they got home, the youngest Prince took his goblet to the King so that he might drink of the water which was to make him well; but after drinking only a few drops of the sea-water he became more ill than ever. As he was bewailing himself, his two elder sons came to him and accused the youngest of trying to poison him, and said that they had the real Water of Life, and gave him some. No sooner had he drunk it than he felt better, and he soon became as strong and well as he had been in his youth.

Then the two went to their youngest brother, and mocked him, saying, "It was you who found the Water of Life: you had all the trouble, while we have the reward. You should have been wiser, and kept your eyes open; we stole it from you while you were asleep on the ship. When the end of the year comes, one of us will go and bring away the beautiful Princess. But don't dare to betray us. Our father will certainly not believe you, and if you say a single word, you will lose your life; your only chance is to keep silence."

The old King was very angry with his youngest son, thinking that he had tried to take his life. So he had the Court assembled to give judgement upon him, and it was decided that he must be secretly got out of the way.

One day when the Prince was going out hunting, thinking no evil, the King's Huntsman was ordered to go with him. Seeing the Huntsman look sad, the Prince said to him, "My good Huntsman, what is the matter with you?"

The Huntsman answered, "I can't bear to tell you, and yet I must."

The Prince said, "Say it out; whatever it is I will forgive you."

"Alas!" said the Huntsman. "I am to shoot you dead; it is the King's command."

The Prince was horror-stricken, and said, "Dear Huntsman, do not kill me, give me my life. Let me have your dress, and you shall have my royal robes."

The Huntsman said, "I will gladly do so; I could never have shot you." So they changed clothes, and the Huntsman went home, but the Prince wandered away into the forest.

After a time three waggon loads of gold and precious stones came to the King for his youngest son. They were sent by the Kings who had been saved by the Prince's sword and his miraculous loaf, and who now wished to show their gratitude.

Then the old King thought, What if my son really was innocent? and said to his people, "If only he were still alive! How sorry I am that I ordered him to be killed."

"He is still alive," said the Huntsman. "I could not find it in my heart to carry out your commands," and he told the King what had taken place.

A load fell from the King's heart on hearing the good news, and he sent out a proclamation to all parts of his kingdom that his son was to come home, where he would be received with great favour.

In the meantime the Princess had caused a road to be made of pure shining gold leading to her castle, and told her people that whoever came riding straight along it be the true bridegroom, and they were to admit him. But anyone who came on either one side of the road or the other would not be the right one, and he was not to be let in.

When the year had almost passed, the eldest Prince thought that he would hurry to the Princess, and by giving himself out as her deliverer would gain a wife and a kingdom as well. So he rode away, and when he saw the beautiful golden road, he thought it would be a thousand pities to ride upon it; so he turned aside, and rode to the right of it. But when he reached the gate, the people told him that he was not the true bridegroom, and he had to go away.

"Good Dwarf, can you not tell me where my brothers are?" (page 77).

Soon after, the second Prince came, and when he saw the golden road, he thought it would be a thousand pities for his horse to tread upon it; so he turned aside, and rode up on the left of it. But when he reached the gate, he was also told that he was not the true bridegroom, and, like his brother, was turned away.

When the year had quite come to an end, the third Prince came out of the wood to ride to his beloved, and through her to forget all his past sorrows. So on he went, thinking only of her, and wishing to be with her; and he never even saw the golden road. His horse cantered right along the middle of it, and when he reached the gate, it was flung open and the Princess received him joyfully, and called him her Deliverer, and the Lord of her Kingdom. Their marriage was celebrated without delay, and with much rejoicing. When it was over, she told him that his father had called him back and forgiven him. So he went to him and told him everything: how his brothers had deceived him, and how they had forced him to keep silence. The old King wanted to punish them, but they had taken a ship and sailed away over the sea, and they never *came back as long as they lived.*

The Twelve Dancing Princesses

Jacob and Wilhelm Grimm • Illustrated by Kay Nielsen

Once upon a time there lived in the village of Montignies-sur-Roc a little cow-boy, without either father or mother. His real name was Michael, but he was always called the Star Gazer, because when he drove his cows over the commons to seek for pasture, he went along with his head in the air, gaping at nothing.

As he had a white skin, blue eyes, and hair that curled all over his head, the village girls used to cry after him, "Well, Star Gazer, what are you doing?" and Michael would answer, "Oh, nothing," and go on his way without even turning to look at them.

The fact was that he thought them very ugly, with their sun-burnt necks, their great red hands, their coarse petticoats, and their wooden shoes. He had heard that somewhere in the world there were girls whose necks were white and whose hands were small, who were always dressed in the finest silks and laces, and were called Princesses, and while his companions round the fire saw nothing in the flames but common everyday fancies, he dreamed that he had the happiness to marry a Princess.

One morning about the middle of August, just at mid-day when the sun was hottest, Michael ate his dinner of a piece of dry bread, and went to sleep under an oak. And while he slept he dreamt that there appeared before him a beautiful Lady, dressed in a robe of cloth of gold, who said to him: "Go to the castle of Belœil, and there you shall marry a Princess."

That evening the little cow-boy, who had been thinking a great deal about the advice of the lady in the golden dress, told his dream to the farm people. But, as was natural, they only laughed at the Star Gazer.

The next day at the same hour he went to sleep again under the same tree. The Lady appeared to him a second time, and said, "Go to the castle of Belœil, and you shall marry a Princess."

In the evening Michael told his friends that he had dreamed the same dream again, but they only laughed at him more than before. Never mind, he thought to himself; if the Lady appears to me a third time, I will do as she tells me.

The following day, to the great astonishment of all the village, about two o'clock in the afternoon a voice was heard singing:

> "Raleô, raleô,
> How the cattle go!"

It was the little cow-boy driving his herd back to the byre.

The farmer began to scold him furiously, but he answered quietly, "I am going away," made his clothes into a bundle, said good-bye to all his friends, and boldly set out to seek his fortune.

There was great excitement through all the village, and on the top of the hill the people stood holding their sides with laughing, as they watched the Star Gazer trudging bravely along the valley with his bundle at the end of his stick.

It was enough to make anyone laugh, certainly.

It was well known for full twenty miles round that there lived in the castle of Belœil twelve Princesses of wonderful beauty, and as proud as they were beautiful, and who were besides so very sensitive and of such truly royal blood that they would have felt at once the presence of a pea in their beds, even if the mattresses had been laid over it.

It was whispered about that they led exactly the lives that Princesses ought to lead, sleeping far into the morning, and never getting up till mid-day. They had twelve beds all in the same room, but what was very extraordinary was the fact that though they were locked in by triple bolts, every morning their satin shoes were found worn into holes.

When they were asked what they had been doing all night, they always answered that they had been asleep; and, indeed, no noise was ever heard in the room, yet the shoes could not wear themselves out alone!

At last the Duke of Belœil ordered the trumpet to be sounded, and a proclamation to be made that whoever could discover how his daughters wore out their shoes should choose one of them for his wife.

On hearing the proclamation a number of Princes arrived at the castle to try their luck. They watched all night behind the open door of the Princesses, but when the morning came, they had all disappeared, and no one could tell what had become of them.

When he reached the castle, Michael went straight to the gardener and offered his services. Now it happened that the garden boy had just been sent away, and though the Star Gazer did not look very sturdy, the gardener agreed to take him, as he thought that his pretty face and golden curls would please the Princesses.

The first thing he was told was that when the Princesses got up he was to present each one with a bouquet, and Michael thought that if he had nothing more unpleasant to do than that he should get on very well.

Accordingly he placed himself behind the door of the Princesses' room, with the twelve bouquets in a basket. He gave one to each of the sisters, and they took them without even deigning to look at the lad, except Lina, the youngest, who fixed her large black eyes as soft as velvet on him, and exclaimed, "Oh, how pretty he is—our new flower boy!" The rest all burst out laughing, and the eldest pointed out that a Princess ought never to lower herself by looking at a garden boy.

Now Michael knew quite well what had happened to all the Princes, but notwithstanding, the beautiful eyes of the Princess Lina inspired him with a violent longing to try his fate. Unhappily he did not dare to come forward, being afraid that he should only be jeered at, or even turned away from the castle on account of his impudence.

Nevertheless, the Star Gazer had another dream. The Lady in the golden dress appeared to him once more, holding in one hand two young laurel-trees, a cherry laurel and a rose laurel, and in the other hand a little golden rake, a little golden bucket, and a silken towel. She thus addressed him:

82

"Plant these two laurels in two large pots, rake them over with the rake, water them with the bucket, and wipe them with the towel. When they have grown as tall as a girl of fifteen, say to each of them, 'My beautiful laurel, with the golden rake I have raked you, with the golden bucket I have watered you, with the silken towel I have wiped you.' Then after that ask anything you choose, and the laurels will give it to you."

Michael thanked the lady in the golden dress, and when he woke he found the two laurel-bushes beside him. So he carefully obeyed the orders he had been given by the lady.

The trees grew very fast, and when they were as tall as a girl of fifteen he said to the cherry laurel, "My lovely cherry laurel, with the golden rake I have raked thee, with the golden bucket I have watered thee, with the silken towel I have wiped thee. Teach me how to become invisible." Then there instantly appeared on the laurel a pretty white flower, which Michael gathered and stuck into his button-hole.

That evening, when the Princesses went upstairs to bed, Michael followed them barefoot, so that he might make no noise, and hid himself under one of the twelve beds, so as not to take up much room.

The Princesses began at once to open their wardrobes and boxes. They took out of them the most magnificent dresses, which they put on before their mirrors, and when they had finished, turned themselves all round to admire their appearances.

Michael could see nothing from his hiding-place, but he could hear everything, and he listened to the Princesses laughing and jumping with pleasure. At last the eldest said, "Be quick, my sisters, our partners will be impatient." At the end of an hour, when the Star Gazer heard no more noise, he peeped out and saw the twelve sisters in splendid garments, with their satin shoes on their feet, and in their hands the bouquets he had brought them.

"Are you ready?" asked the eldest.

"Yes," replied the other eleven in chorus, and they took their places one by one behind her.

Then the eldest Princess clapped her hands three times and a trap door opened. All the Princesses disappeared down a secret staircase, and Michael hastily followed them.

As he was following on the steps of the Princess Lina, he carelessly trod on her dress.

"There is somebody behind me," cried the Princess; "they are holding my dress."

"You foolish thing," said her eldest sister, "you are always afraid of something. It is only a nail which caught you."

They went down, down, down till at last they came to a passage with a door at one end, which was only fastened with a latch. The eldest Princess opened it, and they found themselves immediately in a lovely little wood, where the leaves were spangled with drops of silver which shone in the brilliant light of the moon.

They next crossed another wood, where the leaves were sprinkled with gold, and after that another still, where the leaves glittered with diamonds.

At last the Star Gazer perceived a large lake, and on the shores of the lake twelve little boats with awnings, in which were seated twelve Princes, who, grasping their oars, awaited the Princesses.

Each Princess entered one of the boats, and Michael slipped into that which held the youngest. The boats glided along rapidly, but Lina's, from being heavier, was always behind the rest. "We never went so slowly before," said the Princess. "What can be the reason?"

"I don't know," answered the Prince. "I assure you I am rowing as hard as I can."

On the other side of the lake the garden boy saw a beautiful castle splendidly illuminated, whence came the lively music of fiddles, kettle-drums, and trumpets.

In a moment they touched land, and the company jumped out of the boats; and the Princes, after having securely fastened their barques, gave their arms to the Princesses and conducted them to the castle.

Michael followed, and entered the ball-room in their train. Everywhere were mirrors, lights, flowers, and damask hangings.

The Star Gazer was quite bewildered at the magnificence of the sight.

He placed himself out of the way in a corner, admiring the grace and beauty of the Princesses. Their loveliness was of every kind. Some were fair and some were dark; some had chestnut hair, or curls darker still, and some had golden locks. Never were so many beautiful Princesses seen together at one time, but the one whom the cow-boy thought the most beautiful and most fascinating was the little Princess with the velvet eyes.

With what eagerness she danced! Leaning on her partner's shoulder, she swept by like a whirlwind. Her cheeks flushed, her eyes sparkled, and it was plain that she loved dancing better than anything else.

The poor boy envied those handsome young men with whom she danced so gracefully, but he did not know how little reason he had to be jealous of them.

The young men were really the Princes who, to the number of fifty at least, had tried to steal the Princesses' secret. The Princesses had made them drink something of a philtre, which froze the heart and left nothing but the love of dancing.

They danced on till the shoes of the Princesses were worn into holes. When the cock crowed the third time the fiddles stopped, and a delicious supper was served, consisting of sugared orange flowers, crystallised rose leaves, powdered violets, cracknels, wafers, and other dishes, which are, as everyone knows, the favourite food of Princesses.

After supper the dancers all went back to their boats, and this time the Star Gazer entered that of the eldest Princess. They crossed again the wood with the diamond-spangled leaves, the wood with gold-sprinkled leaves, and the wood whose leaves glittered with drops of silver, and as a proof of what he had seen, the boy broke a small branch from a tree in the last wood. Lina turned as she heard the noise made by the breaking of the branch.

"What was that noise?" she said.

"It was nothing," replied her eldest sister; "it was only the screech of the barn-owl that roosts in one of the turrents of the castle."

While she was speaking, Michael managed to slip in front, and running up the staircase, he reached the Princesses' room first. He flung open the window, and sliding down the vine which climbed up the wall, found himself in the garden just as the sun was beginning to rise and it was time for him to set to his work.

That day, when he made up the bouquets, Michael hid the branch with the silver drops in the nosegay intended for the youngest Princess.

When Lina discovered it, she was much surprised. However, she said nothing to her sisters, but as she met the boy by accident while she was walking under the shade of the elms, she suddenly stopped as if to speak to him; then, altering her mind, went on her way.

The same evening the twelve sisters went again to the ball, and the Star Gazer again followed

She suddenly stopped as if to speak to him; then, altering her mind, went on her way.

them and crossed the lake in Lina's boat. This time it was the Prince who complained that the boat seemed very heavy.

"It is the heat," replied the Princess. "I, too, have been feeling very warm."

During the ball she looked everywhere for the gardener's boy, but she never saw him.

As they came back, Michael gathered a branch from the wood with the gold-spangled leaves, and now it was the eldest Princess who heard the noise that it made in breaking.

"It is nothing," said Lina; "only the cry of the owl which roosts in the turrets of the castle."

As soon as she got up she found the branch in her bouquet. When the sisters went down she stayed a little behind and said to the cow-boy, "Where does this branch come from?"

"Your Royal Highness knows well enough," answered Michael.

"So you have followed us?"

"Yes, Princess."

"How did you manage it? We never saw you."

"I hid myself," replied the Star Gazer quietly.

The Princess was silent a moment, and then said, "You know our secret! Keep it. Here is the reward of your discretion." And she flung the boy a purse of gold.

"I do not sell my silence," answered Michael, and he went away without picking up the purse.

For three nights Lina neither saw nor heard anything extraordinary; on the fourth she heard a rustling among the diamond-spangled leaves of the wood. That day there was a branch of the trees in her bouquet.

She took the Star Gazer aside, and said to him in a harsh voice, "You know what price my father has promised to pay for our secret?"

"I know, Princess," answered Michael.

"Don't you mean to tell him?"

"That is not my intention."

"Are you afraid?"

"No, Princess."

"What makes you so discreet then?"

But Michael was silent.

Lina's sisters had seen her talking to the little garden boy, and jeered at her for it.

"What prevents your marrying him?" asked the eldest. "You would become a gardener, too; it is a charming profession. You could live in a cottage at the end of the park, and help your husband to draw up water from the well, and when we get up, you could bring us our bouquets."

The Princess Lina was very angry, and when the Star Gazer presented her bouquet, she received it in a disdainful manner.

Michael behaved most respectfully. He never raised his eyes to her, but nearly all day she felt him at her side without ever seeing him.

One day she made up her mind to tell everything to her eldest sister.

"What!" said she. "This rogue knows our secret, and you never told me! I must lose no time in getting rid of him."

"But how?"

"Why, by having him taken to the tower with the dungeons, of course."

For this was the way that in old times beautiful Princesses got rid of people who knew too much.

But the astonishing part of it was that the youngest sister did not seem at all to relish this

method of stopping the mouth of the gardener's boy, who, after all, had said nothing to their father.

It was agreed that the question should be submitted to the other ten sisters. All were on the side of the eldest. Then the youngest sister declared that if they laid a finger on the little garden boy, she would herself go and tell their father the secret of the holes in their shoes.

At last it was decided that Michael should be put to the test: that they would take him to the ball, and at the end of supper would give him the philtre which was to enchant him like the rest.

They sent for the Star Gazer, and asked him how he had contrived to learn their secret; but still he remained silent.

Then, in commanding tones, the eldest sister gave him the order they had agreed upon.

He only answered, "I will obey."

He had really been present, invisible, at the council of Princesses, and had heard all; but he had make up his mind to drink of the philtre, and sacrifice himself to the happiness of her he loved.

Not wishing, however, to cut a poor figure at the ball by the side of the other dancers, he went at once to the laurels, and said:

"My lovely rose laurel, with the golden rake I have raked thee, with the golden bucket I have watered thee, with a silken towel I have dried thee. Dress me like a prince."

A beautiful pink flower appeared. Michael gathered it, and found himself in a moment clothed in velvet, which was as black as the eyes of the little Princess, with a cap to match, a diamond aigrette, and a blossom of the rose laurel in his button-hole.

Thus dressed he presented himself that evening before the Duke of Belœil, and obtained leave to try and discover his daughters' secret. He looked so distinguished that hardly anyone would have known who he was.

The twelve Princesses went upstairs to bed. Michael followed them, and waited behind the open door till they gave the signal for departure.

This time he did not cross in Lina's boat. He gave his arm to the eldest sister, danced with each in turn, and was so graceful that everyone was delighted with him. At last the time came for him to dance with the little Princess. She found him the best partner in the world, but he did not dare to speak a single word to her.

When he was taking her back to her place, she said to him in a mocking voice, "Here you are at the summit of your wishes: you are being treated like a Prince."

"Don't be afraid," replied the Star Gazer gently. "You shall never be a gardener's wife."

The little Princess stared at him with a frightened face, and he left her without waiting for an answer.

When the satin slippers were worn through, the fiddles stopped, and the dinner table was set. Michael was placed next to the eldest sister, and opposite the youngest.

They gave him the most exquisite dishes to eat, and the most delicate wines to drink; and in order to turn his head more completely, compliments and flattery were heaped on him from every side.

But he took care not to be intoxicated, either by the wine or the compliments.

At last the eldest sister made a sign, and one of the pages brought in a large golden cup.

"The enchanted castle has no more secrets for you," she said to the Star Gazer. "Let us drink to your triumph."

He cast a lingering glance at the little Princess, and without hesitation lifted the cup.

"Don't drink!" suddenly cried out the little Princess. "I would rather marry a gardener."

And she burst into tears.

Michael flung the contents of the cup behind him, sprang over the table, and fell at Lina's feet. The rest of the Princes fell likewise at the knees of the Princesses, each of whom chose a husband and raised him to her side. The charm was broken.

The twelve couples embarked in the boats, which crossed back many times in order to carry over the other Princes. Then they all went through the three woods, and when they had passed the door of the underground passage, a great noise was heard, as if the enchanted castle were crumbling to the earth.

They went straight to the room of the Duke of Belœil, who had just awoke. Michael held in his hand the golden cup, and he revealed the secret of the holes in the shoes.

"Choose, then," said the Duke, "whichever you prefer."

"My choice is already made," replied the garden boy, and he offered his hand to the youngest Princess, who blushed and lowered her eyes.

The Princess Lina did not become a gardener's wife; on the contrary, it was the Star Gazer who became a Prince: but before the marriage ceremony the Princess insisted that her lover should tell her how he came to discover the secret.

So he showed her the two laurels which had helped him, and she, like a prudent girl, thinking they gave him too much advantage over his wife, cut them off at the root and threw them in the fire.

And this is why the country girls go about singing,

> *"Nous n'irons plus au bois,*
> *Les lauriers sont coupés,"*

and dancing in summer by the light of the moon.

"Don't drink!" suddenly cried out the little Princess. "I would rather marry a gardener."

88

Cinderella

Charles Perrault • Illustrated by Arthur Rackham

There was once an honest gentleman who took for his second wife a lady, the proudest and most disagreeable in the whole country. She had two daughters exactly like herself in all things. He also had one little girl, who resembled her dead mother, the best woman in all the world. Scarcely had the second marriage taken place than the stepmother became jealous of the good qualities of the little girl, who was so great a contrast to her own two daughters. She gave her all the menial occupations of the house—compelled her to wash the floors and staircases, to dust the bedrooms, and clean the grates; and while her sisters occupied carpeted chambers hung with mirrors, where they could see themselves from head to foot, this poor little damsel was sent to sleep in an attic, on an old straw mattress, with only one chair and not a looking-glass in the room.

She suffered all in silence, not daring to complain to her father, who was entirely ruled by his new wife. When her daily work was done, she sat down in the chimney-corner among the ashes;

She had two daughters exactly like herself in all things.

She sat down in the chimney-corner among the ashes.

from which the two sisters gave her the nickname of Cinderella. But Cinderella, however shabbily clad, was handsomer than they were with all their fine clothes.

It happened that the King's son gave a series of balls, to which were invited all the rank and fashion of the city, and among the rest the two elder sisters. They were very proud and happy, and occupied their whole time in deciding what they should wear: a source of new trouble to Cinderella, whose duty it was to get up their fine linen and laces, and who never could please them however much she tried. They talked of nothing but their clothes.

"I," said the elder, "shall wear my velvet gown and my trimmings of English lace."

"And I," added the younger, "will have but my ordinary silk petticoat, but I shall adorn it with an upper skirt of flowered brocade, and shall put on my diamond tiara, which is a great deal finer than anything of yours."

Here the elder sister grew angry, and the dispute began to run so high that Cinderella, who was known to have excellent taste, was called upon to decide between them. She gave them the best advice she could, and gently and submissively offered to dress them herself, and especially to arrange their hair—an accomplishment in which she excelled many a noted coiffeur. The important evening came, and she exercised all her skill to adorn the two young ladies.

While she was combing out the elder's hair, this ill-natured girl said sharply, "Cinderella, do you not wish you were going to the ball?"

"Ah, madam" (they obliged her always to say "madam"), "you are only mocking me; it is not my fortune to have any such pleasure."

"You are right: people would only laugh to see a little cinder-wench at a ball."

Any other than Cinderella would have dressed the hair all awry; but she was good, and dressed it perfectly even and smooth, and as prettily as she could.

91

The sisters had scarcely eaten for two days, and had broken a dozen stay-laces a day in trying to make themselves slender; but to-night they broke a dozen more, and lost their tempers over and over again before they had completed their toilet. When at last the happy moment arrived, Cinderella followed them to the coach; after it had whirled them away, she sat down by the kitchen fire and cried.

Immediately her Godmother, who was a Fairy, appeared beside her.

"What are you crying for, my little maid?"

"Oh, I wish—I wish—" Her sobs stopped her.

"You wish to go to the ball; isn't it so?"

Cinderella nodded.

"Well, then, be a good girl, and you shall go. First run into the garden and fetch me the largest pumpkin you can find."

Cinderella did not comprehend what this had to do with her going to the ball, but being obedient and obliging she went. Her Godmother took the pumpkin, and having scooped out all its inside, struck it with her wand; it became a splendid gilt coach, lined with rose-coloured satin.

"Now fetch me the mouse-trap out of the pantry, my dear."

Cinderella brought it; it contained six of the fattest, sleekest mice. The Fairy lifted up the wire door, and as each mouse ran out she struck it and changed it into a beautiful black horse.

"But what shall I do for your coachman, Cinderella?"

Cinderella suggested that she had seen a large black rat in the rat-trap, and he might serve for want of better.

"You are right; go and look again for him."

He was found, and the Fairy made him into a most respectable coachman, with the finest coat imaginable. She afterwards took six lizards from behind the pumpkin frame, and changed

She struck it and changed it into a beautiful black horse.

Her ragged frock lengthened into a gown of sweeping satin.

them into six footmen, all in splendid livery, who immediately jumped up behind the carriage, as if they had been footmen all their days.

"Well, Cinderella, now you can go to the ball."

"What, in these clothes?" said Cinderella piteously, looking down on her ragged frock.

Her Godmother laughed, and touched her also with the wand; at which her wretched threadbare jacket became stiff with gold and sparkling with jewels, and her ragged frock lengthened into a gown of sweeping satin, from underneath which peeped out her little feet, no longer bare, but covered with silk stockings and the prettiest glass slippers in the world.

"Now, Cinderella, depart; but remember, if you stay one instant after midnight, your carriage will become a pumpkin, your coachman a rat, your horses mice, and your footmen lizards; while you yourself will be the little cinder-wench you were an hour ago."

Cinderella promised without fear, her heart was so full of joy.

Arrived at the palace, the King's son, whom some one, probably the Fairy, had told to await the coming of an uninvited Princess whom nobody knew, was standing at the entrance, ready to receive her. He offered her his hand, and led her with the utmost courtesy through the assembled guests, who stood aside to let her pass, whispering to one another, "Oh, how beautiful she is!" It might have turned the head of any one but poor Cinderella, who was so used to be despised that she took it all as if it were something happening in a dream.

Her triumph was complete; even the old King said to the Queen that never since Her Majesty's young days had he seen so charming and elegant a person. All the Court ladies scanned her eagerly, clothes and all, determining to have theirs made next day of exactly the same pattern. The King's son himself led her out to dance, and she danced so gracefully that he admired her more and more. Indeed, at supper, which was fortunately early, his admiration quite took away his appetite. As for Cinderella herself, with an involuntary shyness she sought out her sisters, placed herself beside them, and offered them all sorts of civil attentions, which, coming as they supposed from a stranger, and so magnificent a lady, almost overwhelmed them with delight.

While she was talking with them, she heard the clock strike a quarter to twelve; and making a courteous adieu to the royal family, she re-entered her carriage, escorted tenderly by the King's son, and arrived in safety at her own door. There she found her Godmother, who smiled approval, and of whom she begged permission to go to a second ball, the following night, to which the Queen had earnestly invited her.

While she was talking, the two sisters were heard knocking at the gate, and the Fairy Godmother vanished, leaving Cinderella sitting in the chimney-corner, rubbing her eyes and pretending to be very sleepy.

"Ah," cried the eldest sister maliciously, "it has been the most delightful ball; and there was present the most beautiful Princess I ever saw, who was so exceedingly polite to us both."

"Was she?" said Cinderella indifferently. "And who might she be?"

"Nobody knows, though everybody would give their eyes to know, especially the King's son."

"Indeed!" replied Cinderella, a little more interested. "I should like to see her. Miss Javotte"—that was the elder sister's name—"will you not let me go to-morrow, and lend me your yellow gown that you wear on Sundays?"

"What, lend my yellow gown to a cinder-wench! I am not so mad as that." At which refusal Cinderella did not complain, for if her sister really had lent her the gown, she would have been considerably embarrassed.

The next night came, and the two young ladies, richly dressed in different toilets, went to the ball. Cinderella, more splendidly attired and beautiful than ever, followed them shortly after. "Now remember twelve o'clock," was her Godmother's parting speech, and she thought she certainly should. But the Prince's attentions to her were greater even than during the first evening, and in the delight of listening to his pleasant conversation, time slipped by unperceived. While she was sitting beside him in a lovely alcove, and looking at the moon from under a bower of orange blossoms, she heard a clock strike the first stroke of twelve. She started up, and fled away as lightly as a deer.

Amazed, the Prince followed, but could not catch her. Indeed he missed his lovely Princess altogether, and only saw running out of the palace doors a little dirty lass whom he had never beheld before, and of whom he certainly would never have taken the least notice. Cinderella arrived at home breathless and weary, ragged and cold, without carriage, or footmen, or coachman—the only remnant of her past magnificence being one of her little glass slippers; the other she had dropped in the ballroom as she ran away.

When the two sisters returned, they were full of this strange adventure: how the beautiful lady had appeared at the ball more beautiful than ever, and enchanted every one who looked at her; and how, as the clock was striking twelve, she had suddenly risen up and fled through the ballroom, disappearing no one knew how or where, and dropping one of her glass slippers behind her in her flight; how the King's son had remained inconsolable until he chanced to pick up the little glass slipper, which he carried away in his pocket, and was seen to take it out continually and look at it affectionately, with the air of a man very much in love; in fact, from his behaviour during the remainder of the evening, all the court and royal family were convinced that he had become desperately enamoured of the wearer of the little glass slipper.

Cinderella listened in silence, turning her face to the kitchen fire, and perhaps it was that which made her look so rosy; but nobody ever noticed or admired her at home, so it did not signify, and next morning she went to her weary work again just as before.

A few days after, the whole city was attracted by the sight of a herald going round with a little glass slipper in his hand, publishing, with a flourish of trumpets, that the King's son ordered this to be fitted on the foot of every lady in the kingdom, and that he wished to marry the lady whom it fitted best, or to whom it and the fellow-slipper belonged. Princesses, duchesses, countesses, and simple gentlewomen all tried it on, but being a Fairy slipper it fitted nobody; and besides, nobody could produce its fellow-slipper, which lay all the time safely in the pocket of Cinderella's old linsey gown.

At last the herald came to the house of the two sisters, and though they well knew neither of themselves was the beautiful lady, they made every attempt to get their clumsy feet into the glass slipper, but in vain.

"Let me try it on," said Cinderella from the chimney-corner.

"What, you?" cried the others, bursting into shouts of laughter; but Cinderella only smiled, and held out her hand.

Her sisters could not prevent her, since the command was that every young maiden in the city should try on the slipper, in order that no chance might be left untried, for the prince was nearly breaking his heart; and his father and mother were afraid that, though a Prince, he would actually die for love of the beautiful unknown lady.

So the herald bade Cinderella sit down on a three-legged stool in the kitchen, and himself put the slipper on her pretty little foot, which it fitted exactly. She then drew from her pocket the fellow-slipper, which she also put on, and stood up—for with the touch of the magic shoes all her dress was changed likewise—no longer the poor despised cinder-wench, but the beautiful lady whom the King's son loved.

Her sisters recognized her at once. Filled with astonishment, mingled with no little alarm, they threw themselves at her feet, begging her pardon for all their former unkindness. She raised

As the clock was striking twelve she . . . fled through the ballroom . . .

dropping one of her glass slippers behind her in her flight.

and embraced them; told them she forgave them with all her heart, and only hoped they would love her always. Then she departed with the herald to the King's palace, and told her whole story to His Majesty and the royal family, who were not in the least surprised, for everybody believed in Fairies, and everybody longed to have a Fairy Godmother.

For the young Prince, he found her more lovely and lovable than ever, and insisted upon marrying her immediately. Cinderella never went home again, but she sent for her two sisters to the palace, and with the consent of all parties married them shortly afterwards to two rich gentlemen *of the Court.*

She forgave them with all her heart.

The Swineherd

Hans Christian Andersen • Illustrated by Heath Robinson

There was once a poor Prince. He possessed a kingdom which, though small, was yet large enough for him to marry on, and married he wished to be.

Now it was certainly a little audacious of him to venture to say to the Emperor's daughter, "Will you marry me?" But he did venture to say so, for his name was known far and wide. There were hundreds of Princesses who would gladly have said "Yes," but would she say the same?

Well, we shall see.

On the grave of the Prince's father grew a rose-tree, a very beautiful rose-tree. It only bloomed every five years, and then bore but a single rose, but oh, such a rose! Its scent was so sweet that when you smelt it you forgot all your cares and troubles. And he had also a nightingale which could sing as if all the beautiful melodies in the world were shut up in its little throat. This rose and this nightingale the Princess was to have, and so they were both put into silver caskets and sent to her.

The Emperor had them brought to him in the great hall, where the Princess was playing "Here comes a duke a-riding" with her ladies-in-waiting. And when she caught sight of the big caskets which contained the presents, she clapped her hands for joy.

"If only it were a little pussy-cat!" she said. But the rose-tree with the beautiful rose came out.

"But how prettily it is made!" said all the ladies-in-waiting.

"It is more than pretty," said the Emperor, "it is charming!"

But the Princess felt it, and then she almost began to cry.

"Ugh! Papa," she said, "it is not artificial, it is *real!*"

"Ugh," said all the ladies-in-waiting, "it is real!"

Let us see first what is in the other casket before we begin to be angry, thought the Emperor, and there came out the nightingale. It sang so beautifully that one could hardly utter a cross word against it.

"*Superbe! Charmant!*" said the ladies-in-waiting, for they all chattered French, each one worse than the other.

"How much the bird reminds me of the musical snuff-box of the late Empress!" said an old courtier. "Ah yes, it is the same tone, the same execution!"

"Yes," said the Emperor; and then he wept like a little child.

"I hope that this, at least, is not real?" asked the Princess.

"Yes, it is a real bird," said those who had brought it.

"Then let the bird fly away," said the Princess; and she would not on any account allow the Prince to come.

99

But he was nothing daunted. He painted his face brown and black, drew his cap well over his face, and knocked at the door. "Good-day, Emperor," he said. "Can I get a place here as servant in the castle?"

"Yes," said the Emperor, "but there are so many who ask for a place that I don't know whether there will be one for you; but, still, I will think of you. Stay, it has just occurred to me that I want someone to look after the swine, for I have so very many of them."

And the Prince got the situation of Imperial Swineherd. He had a wretched little room close to the pigsties; here he had to stay, but the whole day he sat working, and when evening was come, he had made a pretty little pot. All round it were little bells, and when the pot boiled, they jingled most beautifully and played the old tune:

> *"Where is Augustus dear?*
> *Alas, he's not here, here, here!"*

But the most wonderful thing was that when one held one's finger in the steam of the pot, then at once one could smell what dinner was ready in any fire-place in the town. That was indeed something quite different from the rose.

Now the Princess came walking past with all her ladies-in-waiting, and when she heard the tune, she stood still and her face beamed with joy, for she also could play, "Where is Augustus dear?"

It was the only tune she knew, but that she could play with one finger.

"Why, that is what I play!" she said. "He must be a most accomplished Swineherd! Listen! Go down and ask him what the instrument costs."

And one of the ladies-in-waiting had to go down; but she put on wooden clogs. "What will you take for the pot?" asked the lady-in-waiting.

"I will have ten kisses from the Princess," answered the Swineherd.

"Heaven forbid!" said the lady-in-waiting.

"Yes, I will sell it for nothing less," replied the Swineherd.

"Well, what does he say?" asked the Princess.

"I really hardly like to tell you," answered the lady-in-waiting.

"Oh, then you can whisper it to me."

"He is disobliging!" said the Princess, and went away. But she had only gone a few steps when the bells rang out so prettily:

> *"Where is Augustus dear?*
> *Alas, he's not here, here, here!"*

"Listen!" said the Princess. "Ask him whether he will take ten kisses from my ladies-in-waiting."

"No, thank you," said the Swineherd. "Ten kisses from the Princess, or else I keep my pot."

"That is very tiresome!" said the Princess. "But you must put yourselves in front of me, so that no one can see."

And the ladies-in-waiting placed themselves in front and then spread out their dresses; so the Swineherd got his ten kisses, and she got the pot.

What happiness that was! The whole night and the whole day the pot was made to boil; there

The Princess came walking past.

100

was not a fire-place in the whole town where they did not know what was being cooked, whether it was at the chancellor's or at the shoemaker's.

The ladies-in-waiting danced and clapped their hands.

"We know who is going to have soup and pancakes; we know who is going to have porridge and sausages—isn't it interesting?"

"Yes, very interesting!" said the first lady-in-waiting.

"But don't say anything about it, for I am the Emperor's daughter."

"Oh no, of course we won't!" said everyone.

The Swineherd—that is to say, the Prince (though they did not know he was anything but a true Swineherd)—let no day pass without making something, and one day he made a rattle which, when it was turned round, played all the waltzes, galops, and polkas which had ever been known since the world began.

"But this is *superbe!*" said the Princess as she passed by. "I have never heard a more beautiful composition. Listen! Go down and ask him what this instrument costs; but I won't kiss him again."

"He wants a hundred kisses from the Princess," said the lady-in-waiting who had gone down to ask him.

"I believe he is mad!" said the Princess, and then she went on; but she had only gone a few steps when she stopped.

"One ought to encourage art," she said. "I am the Emperor's daughter! Tell him he shall have, as before, ten kisses; the rest he can take from my ladies-in-waiting."

"But we don't at all like being kissed by him," said the ladies-in-waiting.

"That's nonsense," said the Princess; "and if I can kiss him, you can too. Besides, remember that I give you board and lodging."

So the ladies-in-waiting had to go down to him again.

"A hundred kisses from the Princess," said he, "or each keeps his own."

"Put yourselves in front of us," she said then; and so all the ladies-in-waiting put themselves in front, and he began to kiss the Princess.

"What can that commotion be by the pigsties?" asked the Emperor, who was standing on the balcony. He rubbed his eyes and put on his spectacles. "Why those are the ladies-in-waiting playing their games; I must go down to them."

So he took off his shoes, which were shoes though he had trodden them down into slippers. What a hurry he was in, to be sure!

As soon as he came into the yard, he walked very softly, and the ladies-in-waiting were so busy counting the kisses and seeing fair play that they never noticed the Emperor. He stood on tiptoe.

"What is that?" he said when he saw the kissing; and then he threw one of his slippers at their heads just as the Swineherd was taking his eighty-sixth kiss.

"Be off with you!" said the Emperor, for he was very angry. And the Princess and the Swineherd were driven out of the empire.

Then she stood still and wept; the Swineherd was scolding, and the rain was streaming down.

"Alas, what an unhappy creature I am!" sobbed the Princess. "If only I had taken the beautiful Prince! Alas, how unfortunate I am!"

And the Swineherd went behind a tree, washed the black and brown off his face, threw away his old clothes, and then stepped forward in his splendid dress, looking so beautiful that the Princess was obliged to courtesy.

So all the ladies-in-waiting put themselves in front,
and he began to kiss the Princess.

"I now come to this. I despise you!" he said. "You would have nothing to do with a noble Prince; you did not understand the rose or the nightingale, but you could kiss the Swineherd for the sake of a toy. This is what you get for it!" And he went into his kingdom and shut the door in her face, and she had to stay outside singing:

"*Where's my Augustus dear?
Alas, he's not here, here, here!*"

The Goosegirl

Jacob and Wilhelm Grimm • Illustrated by Arthur Rackham

There was once an old Queen whose husband had been dead for many years, and she had a very beautiful daughter. When she grew up, she was betrothed to a Prince in a distant country. When the time came for the maiden to be sent into this distant country to be married, the old Queen packed up quantities of clothes and jewels, gold and silver, cups and ornaments, and, in fact, everything suitable to a royal outfit, for she loved her daughter very dearly.

She also sent a Waiting-Woman to travel with her, and to put her hand into that of the bridegroom. They each had a horse. The Princess's horse was called Falada, and it could speak.

When the hour of departure came, the old Queen went to her bedroom, and with a sharp little knife cut her finger and made it bleed. Then she held a piece of white cambric under it, and let three drops of blood fall on to it. This cambric she gave to her daughter, and said, "Dear child, take good care of this; it will stand you in good stead on the journey." They then bade each other a sorrowful farewell. The Princess hid the piece of cambric in her bosom, mounted her horse, and set out to her bridegroom's country.

When they had ridden for a time the Princess became very thirsty, and said to the Waiting-Woman, "Get down and fetch me some water in my cup, from the stream. I must have something to drink."

"If you are thirsty," said the Waiting-Woman, "dismount yourself, lie down by the water, and drink. I don't choose to be your servant."

So, in her great thirst, the Princess dismounted, stooped down to the stream and drank, for she might not have her golden cup. The poor Princess said, "Alas!" and the drops of blood answered, "If your mother knew this, it would break her heart."

The royal bride was humble, so she said nothing, but mounted her horse again. Then they rode several miles farther; but the day was warm, the sun was scorching, and the Princess was soon thirsty again.

When they reached a river she called out again to her Waiting-Woman, "Get down, and give me some water in my golden cup!"

She had forgotten all about the rude words which had been said to her. But the Waiting-Woman answered more haughtily than ever, "If you want to drink, get the water for yourself. I won't be your servant."

Being very thirsty, the Princess dismounted, and knelt by the flowing water. She cried, and said, "Ah me!" and the drops of blood answered, "If your mother knew this, it would break her heart."

While she stooped over the water to drink, the piece of cambric with the drops of blood on it fell out of her bosom, and floated away on the stream; but she never noticed this in her great fear. The Waiting-Woman, however, had seen it, and rejoiced at getting more power over the

"Alas, dear Falada, there thou hangest!"   105

bride. She, by losing the drops of blood, had become weak and powerless.

Now, when she was about to mount her horse, Falada, again, the Waiting-Woman said, "By rights, Falada belongs to me; this jade will do for you!"

The poor little Princess was obliged to give way. Then the Waiting-Woman, in a harsh voice, ordered her to take off her royal robes, and to put on her own mean garments. Finally she forced her to swear before heaven that she would not tell a creature at the Court what had taken place. Had she not taken the oath she would have been killed on the spot. But Falada saw all this and marked it.

The Waiting-Woman then mounted Falada and put the real bride on her poor jade, and they continued their journey.

There was great rejoicing when they arrived at the castle. The Prince hurried towards them, and lifted the Waiting-Woman from her horse, thinking she was his bride. She was led upstairs, but the real Princess had to stay below.

The old King looked out of the window and saw the delicate, pretty, little creature standing in the courtyard; so he went to the bridal apartments and asked the bride about her companion, who was left standing in the courtyard, and wished to know who she was.

"I picked her up on the way, and brought her with me for company. Give the girl something to do to keep her from idling."

But the old King had no work for her, and could not think of anything. At last he said, "I have a little lad who looks after the geese; she may help him."

The boy was called little Conrad, and the real bride was sent with him to look after the geese.

Soon after, the false bride said to the Prince, "Dear husband, I pray you do me a favour."

He answered, "That will I gladly."

"Well, then, let the knacker be called to cut off the head of the horse I rode; it angered me on the way."

Really she was afraid that the horse would speak, and tell of her treatment of the Princess. So it was settled, and the faithful Falada had to die.

When this came to the ear of the real Princess she promised the knacker a piece of gold if he would do her a slight service. There was a great dark gateway to the town through which she had to pass every morning and evening. "Would he nail up Falada's head in this gateway so that she might see him as she passed?"

The knacker promised to do as she wished, and when the horse's head was struck off, he hung it up in the dark gateway. In the early morning, when she and Conrad went through the gateway, she said in passing:

"Alas, dear Falada, there thou hangest!"

And the Head answered:

"Alas, Queen's daughter, there thou gangest!
If thy mother knew thy fate,
Her heart would break with grief so great."

Then they passed on out of the town, right into the fields, with the geese. When they reached the meadow, the Princess sat down on the grass and let down her hair. It shone like pure gold, and when little Conrad saw it, he was so delighted that he wanted to pluck some out; but she said:

106

> "Blow, blow, little breeze,
> And Conrad's hat seize.
> Let him join in the chase
> While away it is whirled,
> Till my tresses are curled
> And I rest in my place."

Then a strong wind sprang up, which blew away Conrad's hat right over the fields, and he had to run after it. When he came back, she had finished combing her hair, and it was all put up again; so he could not get a single hair. This made him very sulky, and he would not say another word to her. And they tended the geese till evening, when they went home.

Next morning, when they passed under the gateway, the Princess said:

> "Alas, dear Falada, there thou hangest!"

Falada answered:

> "Alas, Queen's daughter, there thou gangest!
> If thy mother knew thy fate,
> Her heart would break with grief so great."

Again, when they reached the meadows, the Princess undid her hair and began combing it. Conrad ran to pluck some out; but she said quickly:

> "Blow, blow, little breeze,
> And Conrad's hat seize.
> Let him join in the chase
> While away it is whirled,
> Till my tresses are curled
> And I rest in my place."

The wind sprang up and blew Conrad's hat far away over the fields, and he had to run after it. When he came back the hair was all put up again, and he could not pull a single hair out. And they tended the geese till the evening. When they got home Conrad went to the old King, and said, "I won't tend the geese with that maiden again."

"Why not?" asked the King.

"Oh, she vexes me every day."

The old King then ordered him to say what she did to vex him.

Conrad said, "In the morning, when we pass under the dark gateway with the geese, she talks to a horse's head which is hung up on the wall. She says:

> 'Alas, Falada, there thou hangest!'

And the Head answers:

> 'Alas! Queen's daughter, there thou gangest!
> If thy mother knew thy fate,
> Her heart would break with grief so great.' "

Then Conrad went on to tell the King all that happened in the meadow, and how he had to run after his hat in the wind.

The old King ordered Conrad to go out next day as usual. Then he placed himself behind the dark gateway, and heard the Princess speaking to Falada's head. He also followed her into the field, and hid himself behind a bush, and with his own eyes he saw the Goosegirl and the lad come driving the geese into the field. Then, after a time, he saw the girl let down her hair, which glittered in the sun. Directly after this, she said:

> "Blow, blow, little breeze,
> And Conrad's hat seize.
> Let him join in the chase
> While away it is whirled,
> Till my tresses are curled
> And I rest in my place."

Then came a puff of wind, which carried off Conrad's hat, and he had to run after it. While he was away, the maiden combed and did up her hair; and all this the old King observed. Thereupon he went away unnoticed; and in the evening, when the Goosegirl came home, he called her aside and asked why she did all these things.

"That I may not tell you, nor may I tell any human creature; for I have sworn it under the open sky, because if I had not done so, I should have lost my life."

He pressed her sorely, and gave her no peace, but he could get nothing out of her. Then he said, "If you won't tell me, then tell your sorrows to the iron stove there," and he went away.

She crept up to the stove, and, beginning to weep and lament, unburdened herself to it, and said:

"Here I am, forsaken by all the world, and yet I am a Princess. A false Waiting-Woman brought me to such a pass that I had to take off my royal robes. Then she took my place with my bridegroom while I have to do mean service as a Goosegirl. If my mother knew it, she would break her heart."

The old King stood outside by the pipes of the stove, and heard all that she said. Then he came back, and told her to go away from the stove. He caused royal robes to be put upon her, and her beauty was a marvel. The old King called his son, and told him that he had a false bride—she was only a Waiting-Woman; but the true bride was here, the so-called Goosegirl.

The young Prince was charmed with her youth and beauty. A great banquet was prepared, to which all the courtiers and good friends were bidden. The bridegroom sat at the head of the table with the Princess on one side and the Waiting-Woman at the other; but she was dazzled, and did not recognize the Princess in her brilliant apparel.

When they had eaten and drunk and were all very merry, the old King put a riddle to the Waiting-Woman. "What does a person deserve who deceives his master?" telling the whole story, and ending by asking, "What doom does he deserve?"

The false bride answered, "No better than this. He must be put stark naked into a barrel stuck with nails, and be dragged along by two white horses from street to street till he is dead."

"That is your own doom," said the King, "and the judgement shall be carried out."

When the sentence was fulfilled, the young Prince married his true bride, and they ruled their *kingdom together in peace and happiness.*

The Six Swans

Jakob and Wilhelm Grimm • Illustrated by Walter Crane

Once on a time a King was hunting in a great wood, and he pursued a wild animal so eagerly that none of his people could follow him. When evening came he stood still, and looking round him, he found that he had lost his way; and seeking a path, he found none. Then all at once he saw an old woman with a nodding head coming up to him; and it was a Witch.

"My good woman," said he, "can you show me the way out of the wood?"

"Oh yes, my lord King," answered she, "certainly I can; but I must make a condition, and if you do not fulfil it, you will never get out of the wood again, but die there of hunger."

"What is the condition?" asked the King.

"I have a daughter," said the old woman, "who is as fair as any in the world, and if you will take her for your bride, and make her Queen, I will show you the way out of the wood."

The King consented because of the difficulty he was in, and the old woman led him into her little house, and there her daughter was sitting by the fire.

She received the King just as if she had been expecting him, and though he saw that she was very beautiful, she did not please him, and he could not look at her without an inward shudder. Nevertheless, he took the maiden before him on his horse, and the old woman showed him the way, and soon he was in his royal castle again, where the wedding was held.

The King had been married before, and his first wife had left seven children, six boys, and one girl, whom he loved better than all the world, and as he was afraid the stepmother might not behave well to them, and perhaps would do them some mischief, he took them to a lonely castle standing in the middle of a wood. There they remained hidden, for the road to it was so hard to find that the King himself could not have found it, had it not been for a clew of yarn, possessing wonderful properties, that a wise woman had given him; when he threw it down before him, it unrolled itself and showed him the way. And the King went so often to see his dear children, that the Queen was displeased at his absence; and she became curious and wanted to know what he went out into the wood for so often alone. She bribed his servants with much money, and they showed her the secret, and told her of the clew of yarn, which alone could point out the way; then she gave herself no rest until she had found out where the King kept the clew, and then she made some little silk shirts, and sewed a charm in each, as she had learned witchcraft of her mother. And once when the King had ridden to the hunt, she took the little shirts and went into the wood, and the clew of yarn showed her the way. The children, seeing some one in the distance, thought it was their dear father coming to see them, and came jumping for joy to meet him. Then the wicked Queen threw over each one of the little shirts, and as soon as the shirts touched their bodies, they were changed into swans, and flew away through the wood. So the Queen went home very pleased to think she had got rid of her stepchildren; but the Maiden had not run out with her brothers, and so the Queen knew nothing about her. The next day the King went to see his children, but he found nobody but his daughter.

"Where are thy brothers?" asked the King.

"Ah, dear Father," answered she, "they are gone away and have left me behind," and then she told him how she had seen from her window her brothers in the guise of swans fly away through the wood, and she showed him the feathers which they had let fall in the courtyard, and which she had picked up. The King was grieved, but he never dreamt that it was the Queen who had done this wicked deed, and as he feared lest the Maiden also should be stolen away from him, he wished to take her away with him. But she was afraid of the stepmother, and begged the King to let her remain one more night in the castle in the wood.

Then she said to herself, I must stay here no longer, but go and seek for my brothers.

And when the night came, she fled away and went straight into the wood. She went on all that night and the next day until she could go no longer for weariness. At last she saw a rude hut, and she went in and found a room with six little beds in it; she did not dare to lie down in one, but she crept under one and lay on the hard boards and wished for night. When it was near the time of sun-setting, she heard a rustling sound, and saw six swans come flying in at the window. They alighted on the ground, and blew at one another until they had blown all their feathers off, and then they stripped off their swan-skins as if they had been shirts. And the Maiden looked at them and knew them for her brothers, and was very glad, and crept from under the bed. The brothers were not less glad when their sister appeared, but their joy did not last long.

"You must not stay here," said they to her; "this is a robbers' haunt, and if they were to come and find you here, they would kill you."

"And cannot you defend me?" asked the little sister.

"No," answered they, "for we can only get rid of our swan-skins and keep our human shape every evening for a quarter of an hour, but after that we must be changed again into swans."

Their sister wept at hearing this, and said, "Can nothing be done to set you free?"

"Oh no," answered they, "the work would be too hard for you. For six whole years you would be obliged never to speak or laugh, and make during that time six little shirts out of aster-flowers. If you were to let fall a single word before the work was ended, all would be of no good."

And just as the brothers had finished telling her this, the quarter of an hour came to an end, and they changed into swans and flew out of the window.

But the Maiden made up her mind to set her brothers free, even though it should cost her her life. She left the hut, and going into the middle of the wood, she climbed a tree, and there passed the night. The next morning she set to work and gathered asters and began sewing them together. As for speaking, there was no one to speak to, and as for laughing, she had no mind to it; so she sat on and looked at nothing but her work.

When she had been going on like this for a long time, it happened that the King of that country went a-hunting in the wood, and some of his huntsmen came up to the tree in which the Maiden sat. They called out to her, saying, "Who art thou?" But she gave no answer. "Come down," cried they; "we will do thee no harm." But she only shook her head. And when they tormented her further with questions, she threw down to them her gold necklace, hoping they would be content with that. But they would not leave off, so she threw down to them her girdle, and when that was no good, her garters, and one after another everything she had on and could possibly spare, until she had nothing left but her smock.

But all was no good; the huntsmen would not be put off any longer, and they climbed the

The swans came close up to her with rushing wings, and stooped
round her, so that she could throw the shirts over them (page 112).

tree, carried the Maiden off, and brought her to the King. The King asked, "Who art thou? What wert thou doing in the tree?" But she answered nothing. He spoke to her in all the languages he knew, but she remained dumb: but, being very beautiful, the King inclined to her, and he felt a great love rise up in his heart towards her; and casting his mantle round her, he put her before him on his horse, and brought her to his castle. Then he caused rich clothing to be put upon her, and her beauty shone as bright as the morning, but no word would she utter. He seated her by his side at table, and her modesty and gentle mien so pleased him that he said, "This Maiden I choose for wife, and no other in all the world," and accordingly after a few days they were married.

But the King had a wicked stepmother, who was displeased with the marriage, and spoke ill of the young Queen.

"Who knows where the Maid can have come from?" said she. "And not able to speak a word! She is not worthy of a king!"

After a year had passed, and the Queen brought her first child into the world, the old woman carried it away, and marked the Queen's mouth with blood as she lay sleeping. Then she went to the King and declared that his wife was an eater of human flesh. The King would not believe such a thing, and ordered that no one should do her any harm. And the Queen went on quietly sewing the shirts, and caring for nothing else.

The next time that a fine boy was born, the wicked stepmother used the same deceit, but the King would give no credence to her words, for he said, "She is too tender and good to do any such thing, and if she were only not dumb, and could justify herself, then her innocence would be as clear as day."

When for the third time the old woman stole away the new-born child and accused the Queen, who was unable to say a word in her defence, the King could do no other but give her up to justice, and she was sentenced to suffer death by fire.

The day on which her sentence was to be carried out was the very last one of the sixth year of the years during which she had neither spoken nor laughed, to free her dear brothers from the evil spell. The six shirts were ready, all except one which wanted the left sleeve. And when she was led to the pile of wood, she carried the six shirts on her arm, and when she mounted the pile and the fire was about to be kindled, all at once she cried out aloud, for there were six swans coming flying through the air; and she saw that her deliverance was near, and her heart beat for joy. The swans came close up to her with rushing wings, and stooped round her, so that she could throw the shirts over them; and when that had been done the swan-skins fell off them, and her brothers stood before her in their own bodies quite safe and sound; but as one shirt wanted the left sleeve, so the youngest brother had a swan's wing instead of a left arm.

They embraced and kissed each other, and the Queen went up to the King, who looked on full of astonishment, and began to speak to him and to say, "Dearest husband, now I may dare to speak and tell you that I am innocent, and have been falsely accused," and she related to him the treachery of the stepmother, who had taken away the three children and hidden them. However, the children were soon fetched safely back, to the great joy of the King, and the wicked stepmother was tied to the stake and burnt to ashes.

And the King and Queen lived many years with their children and the Queen's six brothers in peace and joy.

The Happy Prince

Oscar Wilde • Illustrated by Walter Crane

High above the city, on a tall column, stood the statue of the Happy Prince. He was gilded all over with thin leaves of fine gold, for eyes he had two bright sapphires, and a large red ruby glowed on his sword-hilt.

He was very much admired indeed. "He is as beautiful as a weathercock," remarked one of the Town Councillors who wished to gain a reputation for having artistic tastes; "only not quite so useful," he added, fearing lest people should think him unpractical, which he really was not.

"Why can't you be like the Happy Prince?" asked a sensible mother of her little boy who was crying for the moon. "The Happy Prince never dreams of crying for anything."

"I am glad there is some one in the world who is quite happy," muttered a disappointed man as he gazed at the wonderful statue.

"He looks just like an angel," said the Charity Children as they came out of the cathedral in their bright scarlet cloaks and their clean white pinafores.

"How do you know?" said the Mathematical Master. "You have never seen one."

"Ah, but we have, in our dreams!" answered the children; and the Mathematical Master frowned and looked very severe, for he did not approve of children dreaming.

One night there flew over the city a little Swallow. His friends had gone away to Egypt six weeks before, but he had stayed behind, for he was in love with the most beautiful Reed. He had met her early in the spring as he was flying down the river after a big yellow moth, and had been so attracted by her slender waist that he had stopped to talk to her.

"Shall I love you?" said the Swallow, who liked to come to the point at once, and the Reed made him a low bow. So he flew round and round her, touching the water with his wings and making silver ripples. This was his courtship, and it lasted all through the summer.

"It is a ridiculous attachment," twittered the other swallows; "she has no money, and far too many relations"; and indeed the river was quite full of reeds. Then, when the autumn came, they all flew away.

After they had gone, he felt lonely, and began to tire of his lady-love. "She has no conversation," he said, "and I am afraid that she is a coquette, for she is always flirting with the wind." And certainly, whenever the wind blew, the Reed made the most graceful curtsies. "I admit that she is domestic," he continued, "but I love travelling, and my wife, consequently, should love travelling also."

"Will you come away with me?" he said finally to her; but the Reed shook her head, she was so attached to her home.

"You have been trifling with me," he cried; "I am off to the Pyramids. Good-bye!" and he flew away.

All day long he flew, and at night-time he arrived at the city. "Where shall I put up?" he said. "I hope the town has made preparations."

Then he saw the statue on the tall column. "I will put up there," he cried; "it is a fine position with plenty of fresh air." So he alighted just between the feet of the Happy Prince.

"I have a golden bedroom," he said softly to himself as he looked round, and he prepared to go to sleep; but just as he was putting his head under his wing, a large drop of water fell on him. "What a curious thing!" he cried. "There is not a single cloud in the sky, the stars are quite clear and bright, and yet it is raining. The climate in the north of Europe is really dreadful. The Reed used to like the rain, but that was merely her selfishness."

Then another drop fell.

"What is the use of a statue if it cannot keep the rain off?" he said. "I must look for a good chimney-pot," and he determined to fly away.

But before he had opened his wings, a third drop fell, and he looked up, and saw— Ah! What did he see?"

The eyes of the Happy Prince were filled with tears, and tears were running down his golden cheeks. His face was so beautiful in the moonlight that the little Swallow was filled with pity.

"Who are you?" he said.

"I am the Happy Prince."

"Why are you weeping then?" asked the Swallow. "You have quite drenched me."

"When I was alive and had a human heart," answered the statue, "I did not know what tears were, for I lived in the Palace of Sans-Souci, where sorrow is not allowed to enter. In the daytime I played with my companions in the garden, and in the evening I led the dance in the Great Hall. Round the garden ran a very lofty wall, but I never cared to ask what lay beyond it, everything about me was so beautiful. My courtiers called me the Happy Prince, and happy indeed I was if pleasure be happiness. So I lived, and so I died. And now that I am dead they have set me up here so high that I can see all the ugliness and all the misery of my city, and though my heart is made of lead, yet I cannot choose but weep."

"What, is he not solid gold?" said the Swallow to himself. He was too polite to make any personal remarks out loud.

"Far away," continued the statue in a low musical voice, "far away in a little street there is a poor house. One of the windows is open, and through it I can see a woman seated at a table. Her face is thin and worn, and she has coarse, red hands, all pricked by the needle, for she is a seamstress. She is embroidering passion-flowers on a satin gown for the loveliest of the Queen's maids-of-honour to wear at the next Court-ball. In a bed in the corner of the room her little boy is lying ill. He has a fever, and is asking for oranges. His mother has nothing to give him but river water, so he is crying. Swallow, Swallow, little Swallow, will you not bring her the ruby out of my sword-hilt? My feet are fastened to this pedestal and I cannot move."

"I am waited for in Egypt," said the Swallow. "My friends are flying up and down the Nile, and talking to the large lotus-flowers. Soon they will go to sleep in the tomb of the great King. The King is there himself in his painted coffin. He is wrapped in yellow linen, and embalmed with spices. Round his neck is a chain of pale green jade, and his hands are like withered leaves."

"Swallow, Swallow, little Swallow," said the Prince, "will you not stay with me for one night, and be my messenger? The boy is so thirsty, and the mother so sad."

"I don't think I like boys," answered the Swallow. "Last summer, when I was staying on the river, there were two rude boys, the miller's sons, who were always throwing stones at me. They never hit me, of course; we swallows fly far too well for that, and besides, I come of a family famous for its agility; but still, it was a mark of disrespect."

But the Happy Prince looked so sad that the little Swallow was sorry. "It is very cold here," he said, "but I will stay with you for one night, and be your messenger."

"Thank you, little Swallow," said the Prince.

So the Swallow picked out the great ruby from the Prince's sword, and flew away with it in his beak over the roofs of the town.

He passed by the cathedral tower, where the white marble angels were sculptured. He passed by the palace and heard the sound of dancing. A beautiful girl came out on the balcony with her lover. "How wonderful the stars are," he said to her, "and how wonderful is the power of love!" "I hope my dress will be ready in time for the State-ball," she answered. "I have ordered passion-flowers to be embroidered on it; but the seamstresses are so lazy."

He passed over the river, and saw the lanterns hanging to the masts of the ships. He passed over the Ghetto, and saw the old Jews bargaining with each other, and weighing out money in copper scales. At last he came to the poor house and looked in. The boy was tossing feverishly on his bed, and the mother had fallen asleep, she was so tired. In he hopped, and laid the great ruby on the table beside the woman's thimble. Then he flew gently round the bed, fanning the boy's forehead with his wings. "How cool I feel," said the boy, "I must be getting better"; and he sank into a delicious slumber.

Then the Swallow flew back to the Happy Prince, and told him what he had done. "It is curious," he remarked, "but I feel quite warm now, although it is so cold."

"That is because you have done a good action," said the Prince. And the little Swallow began to think, and then he fell asleep. Thinking always made him sleepy.

When day broke, he flew down to the river and had a bath. "What a remarkable phenomenon," said the Professor of Ornithology as he was passing over the bridge. "A swallow in winter!" And he wrote a long letter about it to the local newspaper. Every one quoted it, it was full of so many words that they could not understand.

"To-night I go to Egypt," said the Swallow, and he was in high spirits at the prospect. He visited all the public monuments, and sat a long time on top of the church steeple. Wherever he went the Sparrows chirruped, and said to each other, "What a distinguished stranger!" so he enjoyed himself very much.

When the moon rose, he flew back to the Happy Prince. "Have you any commissions for Egypt?" he cried. "I am just starting."

"Swallow, Swallow, little Swallow," said the Prince, "will you not stay with me one night longer?"

"I am waited for in Egypt," answered the Swallow. "To-morrow my friends will fly up to the Second Cataract. The river-horse couches there among the bulrushes, and on a great granite throne sits the God Memnon. All night long he watches the stars, and when the morning star shines, he utters one cry of joy, and then he is silent. At noon the yellow lions come down to the water's edge to drink. They have eyes like green beryls, and their roar is louder than the roar of the cataract."

"Swallow, Swallow, little Swallow," said the Prince, "far away across the city I see a young man in a garret. He is leaning over a desk covered with papers, and in a tumbler by his side there is a bunch of withered violets. His hair is brown and crisp, and his lips are red as a pomegranate, and he has large and dreamy eyes. He is trying to finish a play for the Director of the Theatre, but he is too cold to write any more. There is no fire in the grate, and hunger has made him faint."

"I will wait with you one night longer," said the Swallow, who really had a good heart. "Shall I take him another ruby?"

115

"Alas! I have no ruby now," said the Prince; "my eyes are all that I have left. They are made of rare sapphires, which were brought out of India a thousand years ago. Pluck out one of them and take it to him. He will sell it to the jeweller, and buy food and firewood, and finish his play."

"Dear Prince," said the Swallow, "I cannot do that," and he began to weep.

"Swallow, Swallow, little Swallow," said the Prince, "do as I command you."

So the Swallow plucked out the Prince's eye, and flew away to the student's garret. It was easy enough to get in, as there was a hole in the roof. Through this he darted, and came into the room. The young man had his head buried in his hands, so he did not hear the flutter of the bird's wings, and when he looked up, he found the beautiful sapphire lying on the withered violets.

"I am beginning to be appreciated," he cried; "this is from some great admirer. Now I can finish my play," and he looked quite happy.

The next day the Swallow flew down to the harbour. He sat on the mast of a large vessel and watched the sailors hauling big chests out of the hold with ropes. "Heave a-hoy!" they shouted as each chest came up. "I am going to Egypt!" cried the Swallow, but nobody minded, and when the moon rose, he flew back to the Happy Prince.

"I am come to bid you good-bye," he cried.

"Swallow, Swallow, little Swallow," said the Prince, "will you not stay with me one night longer?"

"It is winter," answered the Swallow, "and the chill snow will soon be here. In Egypt the sun is warm on the green palm-trees, and the crocodiles lie in the mud and look lazily about them. My companions are building a nest in the Temple of Baalbec, and the pink and white doves are watching them, and cooing to each other. Dear Prince, I must leave you, but I will never forget you, and next spring I will bring you back two beautiful jewels in place of those you have given away. The ruby shall be redder than a red rose, and the sapphire shall be as blue as the great sea."

"In the square below," said the Happy Prince, "there stands a little match-girl. She has let her matches fall in the gutter, and they are all spoiled. Her father will beat her if she does not bring home some money, and she is crying. She has no shoes or stockings, and her little head is bare. Pluck out my other eye, and give it to her, and her father will not beat her."

"I will stay with you one night longer," said the Swallow, "but I cannot pluck out your eye. You would be quite blind then."

"Swallow, Swallow, little Swallow," said the Prince, "do as I command you."

So he plucked out the Prince's other eye, and darted down with it. He swooped past the match-girl, and slipped the jewel into the palm of her hand. "What a lovely bit of glass," cried the little girl; and she ran home, laughing.

Then the Swallow came back to the Prince. "You are blind now," he said, "so I will stay with you always."

"No, little Swallow," said the poor Prince, "you must go away to Egypt."

"I will stay with you always," said the Swallow, and he slept at the Prince's feet.

All the next day he sat on the Prince's shoulder, and told him stories of what he had seen in strange lands. He told him of the red ibises, who stand in long rows on the banks of the Nile, and catch gold fish in their beaks; of the Sphinx, who is as old as the world itself, and lives in the desert, and knows everything; of the merchants, who walk slowly by the side of their camels, and carry amber beads in their hands; of the King of the Mountains of the Moon, who is as black as ebony, and worships a large crystal; of the great green snake that sleeps in a palm-tree, and has twenty priests to feed it with honey-cakes; and of the pygmies who sail over a big lake on large flat leaves, and are always at war with the butterflies.

"Dear little Swallow," said the Prince, "you tell me of marvellous things, but more marvellous

"Swallow, Swallow, little Swallow," said the Prince, "will you not stay with me one night longer?"

than anything is the suffering of men and of women. There is no Mystery so great as Misery. Fly over my city, little Swallow, and tell me what you see there."

So the Swallow flew over the great city, and saw the rich making merry in their beautiful houses, while the beggars were sitting at the gates. He flew into dark lanes, and saw the white faces of starving children looking out listlessly at the black streets. Under the archway of a bridge two little boys were lying in one another's arms to try and keep themselves warm. "How hungry we are!" they said. "You must not lie here," shouted the Watchman, and they wandered out into the rain.

Then he flew back and told the Prince what he had seen.

"I am covered with fine gold," said the Prince, "you must take it off, leaf by leaf, and give it to my poor; the living always think that gold can make them happy."

Leaf after leaf of the fine gold the Swallow picked off, till the Happy Prince looked quite dull and grey. Leaf after leaf of the fine gold he brought to the poor, and the children's faces grew rosier, and they laughed and played games in the street. "We have bread now!" they cried.

Then the snow came, and after the snow came the frost. The streets looked as if they were made of silver, they were so bright and glistening; long icicles like crystal daggers hung down from the eaves of the houses, everybody went about in furs, and the little boys wore scarlet caps and skated on the ice.

The poor little Swallow grew colder and colder, but he would not leave the Prince, he loved him too well. He picked up crumbs outside the baker's door when the baker was not looking, and tried to keep himself warm by flapping his wings.

But at last he knew that he was going to die. He had just strength to fly up to the Prince's shoulder once more. "Good-bye, dear Prince!" he murmured. "Will you let me kiss your hand?"

"I am glad that you are going to Egypt at last, little Swallow," said the Prince, "you have stayed too long here; but you must kiss me on the lips, for I love you."

"It is not to Egypt that I am going," said the Swallow. "I am going to the House of Death. Death is the brother of Sleep, is he not?"

And he kissed the Happy Prince on the lips, and fell down dead at his feet.

At that moment a curious crack sounded inside the statue, as if something had broken. The fact is that the leaden heart had snapped right in two. It certainly was a dreadfully hard frost.

Early the next morning the Mayor was walking in the square below in company with the Town Councillors. As they passed the column he looked up at the statue. "Dear me! How shabby the Happy Prince looks!" he said.

"How shabby indeed!" cried the Town Councillors, who always agreed with the Mayor, and they went up to look at it.

"The ruby has fallen out of his sword, his eyes are gone, and he is golden no longer," said the Mayor; "in fact, he is little better than a beggar!"

"Little better than a beggar," said the Town Councillors.

"And here is actually a dead bird at his feet!" continued the Mayor. "We must really issue a proclamation that birds are not to be allowed to die here." And the Town Clerk made a note of the suggestion.

So they pulled down the statue of the Happy Prince. "As he is no longer beautiful he is no longer useful," said the Art Professor at the University.

Then they melted the statue in a furnace, and the Mayor held a meeting of the Corporation to decide what was to be done with the metal. "We must have another statue, of course," he said, "and it shall be a statue of myself."

"Of myself," said each of the Town Councillors, and they quarrelled. When I last heard of them they were quarrelling still.

"What a strange thing!" said the overseer of the workmen at the foundry. "This broken lead heart will not melt in the furnace. We must throw it away." So they threw it on a dust-heap where the dead Swallow was also lying.

"Bring me the two most precious things in the city," said God to one of His Angels; and the Angel brought Him the leaden heart and the dead bird.

"You have rightly chosen," said God, "for in my garden of Paradise this little bird shall sing *for evermore, and in my city of gold the Happy Prince shall praise me.*"

The Pied Piper

After Charles Marelles • Illustrated by Kate Greenaway

A very long time ago Hamelin town in Brunswick was invaded by bands of rats, the like of which had never been seen before.

They were great black creatures that ran boldly in broad day-light through the streets, and swarmed so, all over the houses, that people at last could not put their hand or foot down anywhere without touching one. When dressing in the morning, they found them in their breeches and petti-coats, in their pockets and in their boots; and when they wanted a morsel to eat, the rats had swept away everything from cellar to garret. The night was even worse. As soon as the lights were out, these nibblers set untiringly to work. Everywhere, in the ceilings, in the floors, in the cupboards, at the doors, there was a chase and a rummage, and so furious a noise of gimlets, pincers, and saws, that not even a deaf man could have rested.

Neither cats nor dogs, nor poison nor traps, nor prayers nor candles burnt to all the saints—nothing would do anything. Then one day there arrived in Hamelin a man with a lean face and piercing eyes, dressed in a brown cloak and pointed cap, who played the bagpipes and sang:

> *"Qui vivra verra:*
> *Le voilà,*
> *Le preneur des rats."*

He stopped on the great market-place before the town hall, turned his back on the church and went on with his music, singing:

> "Who lives shall see:
> This is he,
> The ratcatcher."

The town council had just assembled to consider once more this plague, from which no one could save the town.

The stranger sent word to the councillors that, if they would make it worth his while, he would rid them of all their rats before night, down to the very last.

"Then he is a sorcerer!" cried the citizens. "We must beware of him."

The Town Councillor, who was considered clever, reassured them.

Everywhere, in the ceilings, in the floors, in the cupboards, at the doors.

"Sorcerer or no," said he, "if this Pied Piper speaks the truth, it was he who sent us this horrible vermin that he wants to rid us of to-day in return for money. We must therefore learn to catch the devil in his own snares. Leave it to me."

"Leave it to the Town Councillor," said the citizens one to another.

And the stranger was brought before them.

"Before night," said he, "I will rid Hamelin of its rats if you will but pay me a gros a head."

"A gros a head!" cried the citizens in dismay. "But that will come to millions of florins!"

The Town Councillor simply shrugged his shoulders and said to the stranger, "A bargain! To work; the rats will be paid one gros a head as you ask."

When the people of Hamelin heard of the bargain, they too exclaimed, "A gros a head! But this will cost us a deal of money!"

And the stranger was brought before them.

"Leave it to the Town Councillor," said the town council with a malicious air. And the people, seeing little else was to be done but agree, repeated, "Leave it to the Town Councillor."

So it was, later the same day, the stranger re-appeared on the market-place, and placing the pipe to his lips started to play.

It was first a slow, caressing sound, then more and more lively and urgent, and so piercing that it penetrated to the farthest alleys and retreats of the town.

Soon from the bottom of the cellars, the top of the garrets, from all the nooks and crannies of the houses, out come the rats, through the door and into the street; trip, trip, trip, running in file towards the front of the town hall.

When the square was quite full, the Pied Piper faced about, and, still playing briskly, turned towards the river that runs at the foot of the walls of Hamelin town.

Arrived there, he turned round; the rats were following.

"Hop! Hop!" he cried, pointing with his finger to the middle of the stream, where the water whirled and was drawn down as if through a funnel. And hop! hop! without hesitating, the rats

The Pied Piper faced about, and, still playing briskly, turned towards the river.

Then the stranger had begun to walk quickly, and they followed . . .

took the leap, swam straight to the funnel, plunged in head foremost, and disappeared.

The plunging continued thus without ceasing till midnight.

At last, dragging himself with difficulty, came a big rat, white with age, and stopped on the bank.

It was the King of the band.

"Are they all there, friend Blanchet?" asked the Pied Piper.

"They are all there," replied friend Blanchet.

"And how many were they?"

"Nine hundred and ninety thousand, nine hundred and ninety-nine."

"Well reckoned?"

"Well reckoned."

Running, singing, and dancing to the sound of the music.

"Then go and join them, old sire, and *au revoir*."

Whereupon the old white rat sprang in his turn into the river and disappeared.

When the Pied Piper had thus concluded his business, he went to bed at his inn. For the first time during three months the people of Hamelin slept quietly through the night.

The next morning, at nine o'clock, the Piper repaired to the town hall, where the town council awaited him.

"All your rats jumped into the river yesterday," said he to the councillors, "and I guarantee that not one of them comes back. They were nine hundred and ninety thousand, nine hundred and ninety-nine, at one gros a head. Reckon!"

"Let us reckon the heads first. One gros a head is one head the gros. Where are the heads?"

The Piper, not expecting this treacherous stroke, paled with anger, and his eyes flashed fire.

"The heads!" cried he. "If you care about them, go and find them in the river."

"So," replied the Town Councillor, "you refuse to hold to the terms of your agreement? We ourselves could refuse you all payment. But you have been of use to us, and we will not let you go without a recompense. Here are fifty crowns."

"Keep your recompense for yourself," replied the Pied Piper proudly. "If you do not pay me I will be paid by your heirs."

Thereupon he strode from the hall, and left the town without another word.

When the townsfolk heard how the affair had ended, they rubbed their hands, and with no more scruple than their Town Councillor, they laughed over the Piper, who, they said, was caught in his own trap. But what made them laugh above all was his threat of getting paid by their heirs. Ha! They wished that they had only such creditors for the rest of their lives.

Next day, which was a Sunday, they all went gaily to church, thinking that after Mass they would at last be able to eat something good that the rats had not tasted before them.

Never did they suspect the terrible surprise that awaited them on their return home. No children anywhere, they had all disappeared!

"Our children! Where are our poor children?" The cry was soon heard in all the streets. Finally through the east door of the town came three little boys. They were weeping, and this is the story they told:

While the parents were at church, a wonderful music had resounded and all the little boys and girls that had been left at home had gone out, attracted by the magic sounds, and had rushed to the great market-place. There they found the Pied Piper playing his pipes. Then the stranger had begun to walk quickly, and they followed, running, singing, and dancing to the sound of the music, as far as the foot of the mountain just outside the town. At their approach the mountain had opened a little, and the Piper had gone in with them, after which it had closed again. Only the three little ones who told the adventure had remained outside. One was bandy-legged and could not run fast enough; the other, who had left the house in haste, one foot shod the other bare, had hurt himself against a big stone and could not walk without difficulty; the third had arrived in time, but in hurrying to go in with the others had struck so violently against the wall of the mountain that he fell backwards at the moment it closed upon his comrades.

At this story the parents redoubled their lamentations. They ran with pikes and mattocks to the mountain, and searched till evening to find the opening by which their children had disappeared. But to no avail. At last, the night falling, they returned desolate to Hamelin.

The most unhappy of all was the Town Councillor, for he lost three little boys and two pretty little girls. And to crown all, the people of Hamelin overwhelmed him with reproaches, forgetting that the evening before they had all agreed with him.

What had become of all these unfortunate children?

The parents always hoped they were not dead, and that the Pied Piper, who certainly must have come out of the mountain, would have taken them with him to his country. That is why for several years they sent in search of them to different countries, but no one found any trace of the children.

About one hundred and fifty years after the event, when there was no longer one left of the fathers, mothers, brothers, or sisters of that day, there arrived one evening in Hamelin some merchants from Bremen, returning from the East, who asked to speak with the citizens. They told that they, in crossing Hungary, had sojourned in a mountainous country called Transylvania, where the inhabitants spoke only German, while all around them nothing was spoken but Hungarian. These people also declared that they came from Germany, but they did not know how they chanced

to be in this strange country. "Now," said the merchants of Bremen, "these Germans cannot be other than the descendants of the lost children of Hamelin."

The people of Hamelin did not doubt it; and since that day they regard it as certain that the Transylvanians of Hungary are their country folk, whose ancestors, as children, were brought *there by the Pied Piper.*

The Nightingale

Hans Christian Andersen • Illustrated by Harry Clarke

In China, you must know, the Emperor is a Chinaman, and all whom he has about him are Chinamen too. Many years ago, the Emperor's palace was the most splendid in the world; it was made entirely of porcelain, very costly, but so delicate and brittle that one had to take care how one touched it. In the garden were to be seen the most wonderful flowers, and to the costliest of them silver bells were tied, which sounded, so that nobody should pass by without noticing the flowers. Yes, everything in the Emperor's garden was admirably arranged. And it extended so far that the gardener himself did not know where the end was. If a man went on and on, he came into a glorious forest with high trees and deep lakes. The wood extended straight down to the sea, which was blue and deep; great ships could sail to beneath the branches of the trees; and in the trees lived a Nightingale, which sang so splendidly that even the poor fisherman, who had many other things to do, stopped still and listened, when he had gone out at night to throw out his nets, and heard the Nightingale.

"How beautiful that is!" he said; but he was obliged to attend to his property, and thus forgot the bird. But when in the next night the bird sang again, and the fisherman heard it, he exclaimed again, "How beautiful that is!"

From all the countries of the world travellers came to the city of the Emperor, and admired it, and the palace, and the garden, but when they heard the Nightingale, they said, "That is the best of all!"

And the travellers told of it when they came home; and the learned men wrote many books about the town, the palace, and the garden. But they did not forget the Nightingale; that was placed highest of all; and those who were poets wrote most magnificent poems about the Nightingale in the wood by the deep lake.

The books went through all the world, and a few of them once came to the Emperor. He sat in his golden chair, and read, and read; every moment he nodded his head, for it pleased him to peruse the masterly descriptions of the city, the palace, and the garden. "But the Nightingale is the best of all," it stood written there.

"What's that?" exclaimed the Emperor. "I don't know the Nightingale at all! Is there such a bird in my empire, and even in my garden? I've never heard of that. To think that I should have to learn such a thing for the first time from books!"

And hereupon he called his cavalier. This cavalier was so grand that if any one lower in rank then himself dared to speak to him, or to ask him any question, he answered nothing but "P!"— and that meant nothing.

"There is said to be a wonderful bird here called a Nightingale!" said the Emperor. "They say it is the best thing in all my great empire. Why have I never heard anything about it?"

"I have never heard him named," replied the cavalier. "He has never been introduced at Court."

"I command that he shall appear this evening, and sing before me," said the Emperor. "All the world knows what I possess, and I do not know it myself!"

"I have never heard him mentioned," said the cavalier. "I will seek for him. I will find him."

But where was he to be found? The cavalier ran up and down all the staircases, through halls and passages, but no one among all those whom he met had heard talk of the Nightingale. And the cavalier ran back to the Emperor, and said that it must be a fable invented by the writers of books.

"Your Imperial Majesty cannot believe how much is written that is fiction, besides something that they call the black art."

"But the book in which I read this," said the Emperor, "was sent to me by the high and mighty Emperor of Japan, and therefore it cannot be a falsehood. I will hear the Nightingale! It must be here this evening! It has my imperial favour; and if it does not come, all the Court shall be trampled upon after the Court has supped!"

"Tsing-pe!" said the cavalier; and again he ran up and down all the staircases, and through all the halls and corridors; and half the Court ran with him, for the courtiers did not like being trampled upon.

Then there was a great inquiry after the wonderful Nightingale, which all the world knew excepting the people at Court.

At last they met with a poor little girl in the kitchen, who said, "The Nightingale? I know it well; yes, it can sing gloriously. Every evening I get leave to carry my poor sick mother the scraps from the table. She lives down by the strand, and when I get back and am tired, and rest in the wood, then I hear the Nightingale sing. And then the water comes into my eyes, and it is just as if my mother kissed me!"

"Little kitchen-girl," said the cavalier, "I will get you a place in the kitchen, with permission to see the Emperor dine, if you will lead us to the Nightingale, for it is announced for this evening."

So they all went out into the wood where the Nightingale was accustomed to sing; half the Court went forth. When they were in the midst of their journey a cow began to low.

"Oh," cried the Court pages, "now we have it! That shows a wonderful power in so small a creature! I have certainly heard it before."

"No, those are cows lowing!" said the little kitchen-girl. "We are a long way from the place yet."

Now the frogs began to croak in the marsh.

"Glorious!" said the Chinese Court preacher. "Now I hear it—it sounds just like little church bells."

"No, those are frogs!" said the little kitchen-maid. "But now I think we shall soon hear it."

And then the Nightingale began to sing.

"That is it!" exclaimed the little girl. "Listen, listen! And yonder it sits."

And she pointed to a little grey bird up in the boughs.

"Is it possible?" cried the cavalier. "I should never have thought it looked like that! How simple it looks! It must certainly have lost its colour at seeing such grand people around."

"Little Nightingale!" called the little kitchen-maid quite loudly. "Our gracious Emperor wishes you to sing before him."

"With the greatest pleasure!" replied the Nightingale, and began to sing most delightfully.

"It sounds just like glass bells!" said the cavalier. "And look at its little throat, how it's working! It's wonderful that we should never have heard it before. That bird will be a great success at Court."

"Shall I sing once more before the Emperor?" asked the Nightingale, for it thought the Emperor was present.

"My excellent little Nightingale," said the cavalier, "I have great pleasure in inviting you to a Court festival this evening, when you shall charm his Imperial Majesty with your beautiful singing."

"My song sounds best in the green wood!" replied the Nightingale; still it came willingly when it heard what the Emperor wished.

The palace was festively adorned. The walls and the flooring, which were of porcelain, gleamed in the rays of thousands of golden lamps. The most glorious flowers, which could ring clearly, had been placed in the passages. There was a running to and fro, and a thorough draught, and all the bells rang so loudly that one could not hear oneself speak.

In the midst of the great hall, where the Emperor sat, a golden perch had been placed, on which the Nightingale was to sit. The whole Court was there, and the little cook-maid had got leave to stand behind the door, as she had now received the title of a real Court cook. All were in full dress, and all looked at the little grey bird, to which the Emperor nodded.

And the Nightingale sang so gloriously that the tears came into the Emperor's eyes, and the tears ran down over his cheeks; and then the Nightingale sang still more sweetly, which went straight to the heart. The Emperor was so much pleased that he said the Nightingale should have his golden slipper to wear round its neck. But the Nightingale declined this with thanks, saying it had already received a sufficient reward.

"I have seen tears in the Emperor's eyes—that is the real treasure to me. An Emperor's tears have a peculiar power. I am rewarded enough!" Then it sang again with a sweet glorious voice.

"That's the most amiable coquetry I ever saw!" said the ladies who stood round about, and then they took water in their mouth to gurgle when any one spoke to them. They thought they should be nightingales too. And the lackeys and chamber-maids reported that they were satisfied too; and that was saying a good deal, for they are the most difficult to please. In short, the Nightingale achieved a real success.

It was now to remain at Court, to have its own cage with liberty to go out twice every day and once at night. Twelve servants were appointed when the Nightingale went out, each of whom had a silken string fastened to the bird's leg, and which they held very tight. There was really no pleasure in an excursion of that kind.

The whole city spoke of the wonderful bird, and when two people met, one said nothing but "Nightin," and the other said, "gale"; and then they sighed, and understood one another. Eleven pedlars' children were named after the bird, but not one of them could sing a note.

One day the Emperor received a large parcel, on which was written "The Nightingale."

"There we have a new book about this celebrated bird," said the Emperor.

But it was not a book, but a little work of art contained in a box, an artificial nightingale, which was to sing like a natural one, and was brilliantly ornamented with diamonds, rubies, and sapphires. As soon as the artificial bird was wound up, he could sing one of the pieces that he really sang, and then his tail moved up and down, and shone with silver and gold. Round his neck hung a little ribbon, and on that was written, "The Emperor of China's nightingale is poor compared to that of the Emperor of Japan."

"That is capital!" said they all, and he who had brought the artificial bird immediately received the title, Imperial Head-Nightingale-Bringer.

130

"Now they must sing together; what a duet that will be!"

And so they had to sing together; but it did not sound very well, for the real Nightingale sang in its own way, and the artificial bird sang waltzes.

"That's not his fault," said the playmaster; "he's quite perfect, and very much in my style."

Now the artificial bird was to sing alone. He had just as much success as the real one, and then it was much handsomer to look at—it shone like bracelets and breastpins.

Three and thirty times over did it sing the same piece, and yet was not tired. The people would gladly have heard it again, but the Emperor said that the living Nightingale ought to sing something now. But where was it? No one had noticed that it had flown away out of the open window, back to the green wood.

"But what is become of that?" said the Emperor.

And all the courtiers abused the Nightingale, and declared that it was a very ungrateful creature.

"We have the best bird, after all," said they.

And so the artificial bird had to sing again, and that was the thirty-fourth time that they listened to the same piece. For all that, they did not know it quite by heart, for it was so very difficult. And the playmaster praised the bird particularly; yes, he declared that it was better than a nightingale, not only with regard to its plumage and the many beautiful diamonds, but inside as well.

"For you see, ladies and gentlemen, and above all, Your Imperial Majesty, with a real nightingale one can never calculate what is coming, but in this artificial bird everything is settled. One can explain it; one can open it and make people understand where the waltzes come from, how they go, and how one follows up another."

"Those are quite our own ideas," they all said.

And the speaker received permission to show the bird to the people on the next Sunday. The people were to hear it sing, too, the Emperor commanded; and they did hear it, and were as much pleased as if they had all got tipsy upon tea, for that's quite the Chinese fashion; and they all said, "Oh!" and held up their forefingers and nodded. But the poor fisherman, who had heard the real Nightingale, said:

"It sounds pretty enough, and the melodies resemble each other, but there's something wanting, though I know not what!"

The real Nightingale was banished from the country and empire. The artificial bird had its place on a silken cushion close to the Emperor's bed; all the presents it had received, gold and precious stones, were ranged about it; in title it had advanced to be the High Imperial After-Dinner-Singer, and in rank to number one on the left, for the Emperor considered that side the most important on which the heart is placed, and even in an Emperor the heart is on the left side; and the playmaster wrote a work of five and twenty volumes about the artificial bird; it was very learned and very long, full of the most difficult Chinese words; but yet all the people declared that they had read it and understood it, for fear of being considered stupid, and having their bodies trampled on.

So a whole year went by. The Emperor, the Court, and all the other Chinese knew every little twitter in the artificial bird's song by heart. But just for that reason it pleased them best—they could sing with it themselves, and they did so. The street boys sang, "Tsi-tsi-tsi-glug-glug!" and the Emperor himself sang it too. Yes, that was certainly famous.

But one evening, when the artificial bird was singing its best, and the Emperor lay in bed listening to it, something inside the bird said, "Whizz!" Something cracked. "Whir-r-r!" All the wheels ran round, and then the music stopped.

The Emperor immediately sprang out of bed, and caused his body physician to be called; but what could *he* do? Then they sent for a watchmaker, and after a good deal of talking and investigation, the bird was put into something like order; but the watchmaker said that the bird must be carefully treated, for the barrels were worn, and it would be impossible to put new ones in in such a manner that the music would go. There was a great lamentation; only once in a year was it permitted to let the bird sing, and that was almost too much. But then the playmaster made a little speech, full of heavy words, and said this was just as good as before—and so of course it was as good as before.

Now five years had gone by, and a real grief came upon the whole nation. The Chinese were really fond of their Emperor, and now he was ill, and could not, it was said, live much longer. Already a new Emperor had been chosen, and the people stood out in the street and asked the cavalier how their old Emperor did.

"P!" said he, and shook his head.

Cold and pale lay the Emperor in his great gorgeous bed; the whole Court thought him dead, and each one ran to pay homage to the new ruler. The chamberlains ran out to talk it over, and the ladies' maids had a great coffee-party. All about, in all the halls and passages, cloth had been laid down so that no footstep could be heard, and therefore it was quiet there, quite quiet. But the Emperor was not dead yet: stiff and pale he lay on the gorgeous bed with the long velvet curtains and the heavy gold tassels; high up, a window stood open, and the moon shone in upon the Emperor and the artificial bird.

The poor Emperor could scarcely breathe; it was just as if something lay upon his chest. He opened his eyes, and then he saw that it was Death who sat upon his chest, and had put on his golden crown, and held in one hand the Emperor's sword, and in the other his beautiful banner. And all around, from among the folds of the splendid velvet curtains, strange heads peered forth: a few very ugly, the rest quite lovely and mild. These were all the Emperor's bad and good deeds, which stood before him now that Death sat upon his heart.

"Do you remember this?" whispered one to the other. "Do you remember that?" and then they told him so much that the perspiration ran from his forehead.

"I did not know that!" said the Emperor. "Music! Music! The great Chinese drum," he cried, "so that I need not hear all they say!"

And they continued speaking, and Death nodded like a Chinaman to all they said.

"Music! Music!" cried the Emperor. "You little precious golden bird, sing, sing! I have given you gold and costly presents; I have even hung my golden slipper around your neck—sing now, sing!"

But the bird stood still; no one was there to wind him up, and he could not sing without that; but Death continued to stare at the Emperor with his great hollow eyes, and it was quiet, fearfully quiet.

Then there sounded from the window, suddenly, the most lovely song. It was the little live Nightingale, who sat outside on a spray. It had heard of the Emperor's sad plight, and had come to sing to him of comfort and hope. And as it sang the spectres grew paler and paler; the blood ran quicker and more quickly through the Emperor's weak limbs; and even Death listened, and said:

"Go on, little Nightingale, go on!"

"But will you give me that splendid golden sword? Will you give me that rich banner? Will you give me the Emperor's crown?"

And Death gave up each of these treasures for a song. And the Nightingale sang on and on;

The artificial bird had its place on a silken cushion close to the Emperor's bed.

and it sang of the quiet churchyard where the white roses grow, where the elder blossom smells sweet, and where the fresh grass is moistened by the tears of survivors. Then Death felt a longing to see his garden, and floated out at the window in the form of a cold white mist.

"Thanks! Thanks!" said the Emperor. "You heavenly little bird! I know you well. I banished you from my country and empire, and yet you have charmed away the evil faces from my couch, and banished Death from my heart! How can I reward you?"

"You have rewarded me!" replied the Nightingale. "I drew tears from your eyes when I sang the first time—I shall never forget that. Those are the jewels that rejoice a singer's heart. But now sleep and grow fresh and strong again. I will sing you something."

And it sang, and the Emperor fell into a sweet slumber. Ah, how mild and refreshing that sleep was! The sun shone upon him through the windows when he awoke refreshed and restored. Not one of his servants had yet returned, for they all thought he was dead; only the Nightingale still sat beside him and sang.

"You must always stay with me," said the Emperor. "You shall sing as you please; and I'll break the artificial bird into a thousand pieces."

"Not so," replied the Nightingale. "It did well as long as it could; keep it as you have done till now. I cannot build my nest in the palace to dwell in it, but let me come when I feel the wish; then I will sit in the evening on the spray yonder by the window, and sing you something, so that you may be glad and thoughtful at once. I will sing of those who are happy and of those who suffer. I will sing of good and of evil that remain hidden round about you. The little singing bird flies far around, to the poor fisherman, to the peasant's roof, to every one who dwells far away from you and from your Court. I love your heart more than your crown, and yet the crown has an air of sanctity about it. I will come and sing to you—but one thing you must promise me."

"Everything!" said the Emperor; and he stood there in his imperial robes, which he had put on himself, and pressed the sword which was heavy with gold to his heart.

"One thing I beg of you: tell no one that you have a little bird who tells you everything. Then it will go all the better."

And the Nightingale flew away.

The servants came in to look at their dead Emperor, and—yes, there he stood, and the *Emperor said, "Good-morning!"*

Rhymes

Hey Diddle Diddle, the cat and the fiddle. Illustration by Randolph Caldecott.

Ride a Cock-Horse

Illustrated by Randolph Caldecott

Ride a cock-horse
To Banbury Cross,
To see a fine lady
Upon a white horse.
Rings on her fingers,
Bells on her toes,
She shall have music
Wherever she goes.

A Frog He Would A-Wooing Go

Illustrated by Randolph Caldecott

A frog he would a-wooing go,
  Sing, heigho, says Rowley,
Whether his mother would let him or no;
With a rowley, powley, gammon, and spinach,
  Heigho, says Anthony Rowley.

So off he marched with his opera hat,
  Heigho, says Rowley,
And on the way he met with a rat,
  With a rowley, powley, etc.

"Pray, Mr. Rat, will you go with me,"
  Heigho, says Rowley,
"Pretty Miss Mouse for to see?"
  With a rowley, powley, etc.

And when they came to mouse's hall,
  Heigho, says Rowley,
They gave a loud knock, and they gave a loud call,
  With a rowley, powley, etc.

"Pray, Miss Mouse, are you within?"
  Heigho, says Rowley,
"Yes, kind sir, I am sitting to spin,"
  With a rowley, powley, etc.

"Pray, Miss Mouse, will you give us some beer?"
  Heigho, says Rowley,
"For Froggy and I are fond of good cheer,"
  With a rowley, powley, etc.

"Pray, Mr. Frog, will you give us a song?"
  Heigho, says Rowley,
"But let it be something that's not very long."
  With a rowley, powley, etc.

"Indeed, Miss Mouse," replied Mr. Frog,
  Heigho, says Rowley,
"A cold has made me as hoarse as a Hog."
  With a rowley, powley, etc.

"Since you have caught cold," Miss Mouse said,
  Heigho, says Rowley,
"I'll sing you a song that I have just made,"
  With a rowley, powley, etc.

Now while they all were a merry-making,
  Heigho, says Rowley,
The cat and her kittens came tumbling in,
  With a rowley, powley, etc.

The cat she seized the rat by the crown,
  Heigho, says Rowley,
The kittens they pulled the little mouse down,
  With a rowley, powley, etc.

This put poor frog in a terrible fright,
    Heigho, says Rowley,
So he took up his hat and wished them good-night,
    With a rowley, powley, etc.

So there was an end of one, two, and three,
    Heigho, says Rowley,
The rat, the mouse, and the little Frog-ee!
With a rowley, powley, gammon, and spinach,
    Heigho, says Anthony Rowley.

But as Froggy was crossing over a brook,
    Heigho, says Rowley,
A lily-white duck came and gobbled him up,
    With a rowley, powley, etc.

An Uninvited Visitor

By J. G. Sowerby and H. H. Emmerson

Rosie was breakfasting out on the grass,
When two pigs on a walking tour happened to pass.
One pig with rude manners came boldly in front,
And first gave a stare, and then gave a grunt.
As much as to say, "What is that you have got?
Just let me have a taste out of your pot!"
But Rosie said, "Go away, horrid old pig!
I am so little, and *you* are so big!"

Going to See Grandmamma

Written and illustrated by Kate Greenaway

Little Molly and Damon
   Are walking so far,
For they're going to see
   Their kind Grandmamma.

And they very well know,
   When they get there she'll take
From out of her cupboard
   Some very nice cake.

And into her garden
   They know they may run,
And pick some red currants,
   And have lots of fun.

So Damon to doggie
   Says, "How do you do?"
And asks his mamma
   If he may not go too.

The Wind

Robert Louis Stevenson • Illustrated by E. Mars

I saw you toss the kites on high
And blow the birds about the sky;
And all around I heard you pass,
Like ladies' skirts across the grass—
   O wind, a-blowing all day long!
   O wind, that sings so loud a song!

I saw the different things you did,
But always you yourself you hid.
I felt you push. I heard you call,
I could not see yourself at all—
   O wind, a-blowing all day long,
   O wind, that sings so loud a song!

O you that are so strong and cold,
O blower, are you young or old?
Are you a beast of field and tree,
Or just a stronger child than me?
   O wind, a-blowing all day long,
   O wind, that sings so loud a song!

The Sugar-Plum Tree

Eugene Field • Illustrated by Maxfield Parrish

Have you ever heard of the Sugar-Plum Tree?
　'Tis a marvel of great renown!
It blooms on the shore of the Lollipop sea
　In the garden of Shut-Eye Town;
The fruit that it bears is so wondrously sweet
　(As those who have tasted it say)
That good little children have only to eat
　Of that fruit to be happy next day.

When you've got to the tree, you would have a hard time
　To capture the fruit which I sing;
The tree is so tall that no person could climb
　To the boughs where the sugar-plums swing!
But up in that tree sits a chocolate cat,
　And a gingerbread dog prowls below—
And this is the way you contrive to get at
　Those sugar-plums tempting you so:

You say but the word to that gingerbread dog
　And he barks with such terrible zest
That the chocolate cat is at once all agog,
　As her swelling proportions attest.
And the chocolate cat goes cavorting around
　From this leafy limb unto that,
And the sugar-plums tumble, of course, to the ground—
　Hurrah for that chocolate cat!

There are marshmallows, gumdrops, and peppermint canes,
　With stripings of scarlet or gold,
And you carry away of the treasure that rains
　As much as your apron can hold!
So come, little child, cuddle closer to me
　In your dainty white nightcap and gown,
And I'll rock you away to that Sugar-Plum Tree
　In the garden of Shut-Eye Town.

Fables from Aesop

Illustrated by Charles H. Bennett

The Daw in Borrowed Plumes

A rich vulgar Daw, who had a mind to be genteel, tricked herself out in all the gay feathers which fell from the fashionable peacocks, and upon the credit of these borrowed ornaments valued herself above all the birds of the air. But this absurd vanity got her the envy of all the high-born birds with whom she wished to associate; who, indeed, upon the discovery of the truth, by common consent fell to pluming her, and when each bird had taken her own feather, this silly Daw had nothing left wherewith to cover her naked vulgarity.

Fine feathers do not always make fine birds.

The Mole and Her Son

A young conceited Mole one day prevailed upon his mother to take him out of their dwelling-hole to see some of the fine sights so much admired by the people above them. He proceeded to criticise the surrounding beauties.

"What an execrable view this is!" said he, pausing in sight of a beautiful landscape, and twirling his scanty whiskers with an air. "You don't mean to tell me that sky is blue! And the idea of purple grass is positively ridiculous. There's a horse, too, with six legs, and a man taller than his own house. And I'm sure we ought to be able to see the flowers growing on those mountains at this distance! Out of all reason, colour, and proportion. Preposterous!"

"My son, my son," said the mother, "as you are incapable of appreciating what you affect to despise, it is unfortunate that you are not dumb as well as blind, and so might have escaped this exposure of your ignorance."

The fool's tongue is like the rattlesnake's alarm; the providential sign by which we may avoid him.

The Lobster and His Mother

A greenish young Lobster crawling along the Strand with his mother (who, being old and learned, had attained to a deep blue complexion) was struck by the appearance of a specimen of his own tribe whose shell-jacket was of a brilliant red. Young, ignorant, and vain, he viewed the dazzling spectacle with admiration and envy.

"Behold," he said, addressing his parent, "the beauty and splendour of one of our family, thus decked out in glorious scarlet. I shall have no rest till I am possessed of an appearance equally

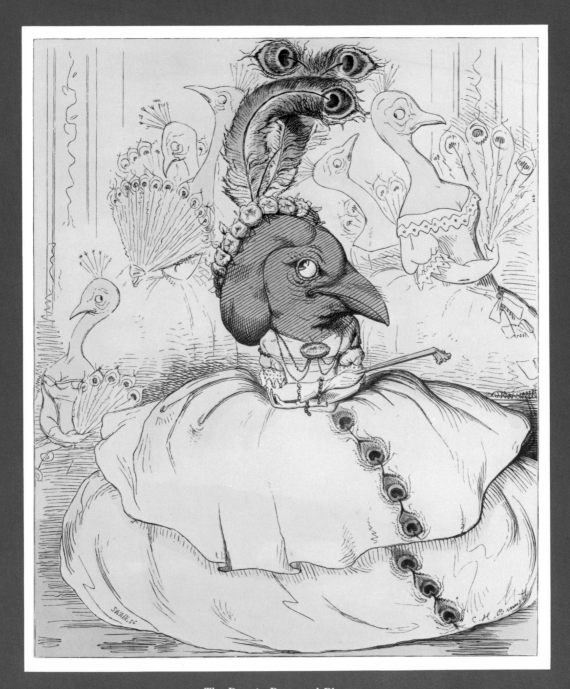

The Daw in Borrowed Plumes.

The Mole and Her Son.

148

The Lobster and His Mother.

149

magnificent. How can I bear to see myself the dingy object I am at present, mingling undistinguished with our race?"

"Proud and heedless idiot," replied the hard old lady, "this same tawdry finery you so earnestly covet is but too easily obtained. In order to possess this appearance *it is only necessary to be boiled.*"

When the Recruiting Sergeant tempts you with the scarlet uniform, he says nothing about getting you into hot water.

The Fox and the Crow

A homely old female Crow, having flown out of a shop in town with a piece of rich cheese in her bill, betook herself to a fine eminence in the country, in order to enjoy it; a cunning Fox, observing, came and sat at her feet, and began to compliment the Crow upon the subject of her beauty.

"I protest," said he, "I never observed it before, but your feathers are of a more delicate white than any I ever saw in my life! Ah, what a fine shape and graceful turn of the body is there! And I make no question but you have a voice to correspond. If it is but as fine as your complexion, I do not know a bird that can pretend to stand in competition with you. Come, let me hear you exercise it by pronouncing a single monosyllable, which will bind me to you, hand and heart, for ever."

The Crow, tickled with this very civil language, nestled and wriggled about, and hardly knew where she was; but thinking the Fox had scarcely done justice to her voice, and wishing to set him right in that matter, she called out "Yes," as loud as possible. But, through this one fatal mistake of opening her mouth, she let fall her rich prize (in the Fox's shrewd estimation all she was worth in the world, which the Fox snapped up directly, and trotted away to amuse himself as he pleased, laughing to himself at the credulity of the Crow, who saw but little of him or her cheese afterwards.

When you listen to a knave's flattery upon what you are, you may have cause to regret not having kept your mouth shut upon what you had.

The Lion and the Gnat

As a great majestic Lion was gathering himself up within his lair to astonish mankind with the wondrous powers of his roar, there came buzzing under his very nose a troublesome Gnat, who challenged him to combat.

"What avail your tremendous lungs and cavernous throat, compared to the melodious pipes of my little organ? And, as for your strength, endurance, and resolution, I defy you to put that point to an issue at once."

The Lion, finding the insect would not be brushed away, was fain to accept the challenge; so to it they went. But the Lion had no chance, for the Gnat charged direct into the drum of the Lion's ear, and there twinged him until in very despair he tore himself with his own paws. In the end the Gnat gained the victory over the noble beast, upon which he flew away, but had the misfortune afterward in his flight to strike into a cobweb, where he, the conqueror, fell a prey to a large Blue-Bottle Spider.

Little miseries are the greatest torments.

The Fox and the Crow.

The Lion and the Gnat.

The Dog in the Manger

A churlish, pampered Cur, who had a comfortable place in a gentleman's Manger well-filled with hay, would snap and snarl to frighten off all poor beasts of draught and burden who passed that way—driven by the hardness of the time of year to beg for food they could not earn by labour in the fields. This Dog wanted for nothing himself, and yet took an ill-natured pleasure in keeping poor hungry creatures from many a meal, which, but for his officious yelping, they might have enjoyed from his Master's bounty.

People will often grudge others what they cannot enjoy themselves.

152

The Dog in the Manger.

NEVER forEVER FOR EVER NEVER

Biographies

Hans Christian Andersen (1805–1875) was born in Odense, Denmark, the son of a poor young shoemaker and an illiterate washerwoman. After his father died in 1816, Hans dropped out of school, yet from these unpromising beginnings he managed to make a fairy-tale legend out of his life as a successful poet, novelist, writer of travel books, and the author of well over a hundred fairy tales of his invention. His first collection, *Tales Told for Children,* was published in Copenhagen in 1835. At first the public was none too enthusiastic, but as further instalments followed in 1836, 1837, 1838, 1845, and frequently thereafter until 1872, the popularity of his fairy stories increased steadily until his name became the household word it has remained to this day.

Jeanne Marie Leprince de Beaumont (1711–1780) was born in Rouen and continued to live in France until about 1747, when, at the end of an unhappy marriage, she went to England to work as a governess. In 1761 she saw one of her dreams fulfilled when the fairy stories she had remembered from her childhood, and had been recounting to her pupils, were published in *The Young Misses Magazine* together with some "useful expositions for the young" which she had also written. Madame de Beaumont's two major contributions to the "magazine"—and to posterity —were "The Three Wishes" and, especially, "Beauty and the Beast," which is represented in this book.

Charles Henry Bennett (1828–1867). Little is known about this important English illustrator except for his major work, *Fables of Aesop, and Others Translated into Human Nature* (1857), from which selections appear on pages 146–53. Bennett illustrated a dozen or so other books, including such varied titles as *Old Nurses Book of Rhymes, Jingles and Ditties* (1858); Bunyan's *The Pilgrim's Progress* (1859); *Nine Lives of a Cat* (1860); Henry Morley's *Oberon's Horn* (1861); *Stories That Little Breeches Told* (1863); and *Lightsome and the Little Golden Lady* (1867).

Eleanor Vere Boyle (1825–1916), known on the title pages of books only by the initials E.V.B., was, in private life, the Honourable Mrs. Robert Boyle, wife of a younger son of the Earl of Cork and Orrery. Her best known works are the illustrations for *Child's Play* (1852); *Beauty and the Beast* (1875); *Fairy Tales by Hans Christian Andersen* (1872); and *A New Child's Play* (1879). In the present book she is represented by "Beauty," by Andersen's "Thumbelina," and by *A New Child's Play,* which provides the charming frontispiece.

E.V.B. [Eleanor Vere Boyle]. From: *A New Child's Play* (Sampson Low), 1879.

Randolph Caldecott (1846–1886) started his professional life as a bank clerk, but at the age of twenty-five he decided to give up the handling of money in favor of the pencil—and was to profit greatly thereby. With no formal training Caldecott nevertheless managed to become, within a few years, the most successful illustrator of children's books since George Cruikshank and Walter Crane—with the possible exception of Kate Greenaway, his exact contemporary and his greatest, and friendliest, rival. Caldecott illustrated at least thirty-six books, sixteen of them in his popular Toy Book Series, from which *A Frog He Would A-Wooing Go* (1883) and *Ride a Cock-Horse* (1884) are presented in this book. "The fewer the lines, the less error committed," Caldecott once said. It is to everyone's regret that his brilliant career was cut short by his early death at the age of forty.

Harry Clarke (1890–1931) grew up in Dublin, and at the age of sixteen worked with his father in a company of stained-glass makers. Later he opened his own shop and executed many notable commissions for church windows, mainly in England and Ireland. He also designed fabrics and illustrated books. His major illustration assignments in the book field were *Fairy Tales by Hans Christian Andersen* (1916), from which the plate on page 133 is taken; Poe's *Tales of Mystery and Imagination* (1919); and *The Fairy Tales of Charles Perrault* (1922). (See colour plate, page 162.)

Randolph Caldecott. From: *Come Lassies and Lads* (Routledge), 1884.

Walter Crane. From: *Goody Two Shoes* (Routledge), 1875.

Walter Crane (1845–1915), a native of Liverpool, became a leading figure in the Arts and Crafts Movement, designing glass, wallpaper, ceramics, and costumes. He was also a painter in the new Pre-Raphaelite tradition, exhibiting at the Royal Academy in 1862 and 1872. He was a prolific illustrator besides. Walter Crane's Toy Books, thirty-nine of them in all, were published between 1865 and 1876. The series included obvious choices such as *Cinderella, Sleeping Beauty, Blue-beard, Beauty and the Beast,* and *The Frog Prince*, from which the color plate on pages 66–67 is reproduced. Crane illustrated some thirty-five other books, including *The Baby's Opera* (1877); various Shakespeare classics, and tales by Mary Louisa Stewart Molesworth; *Household Stories from the Collection of the Bros. Grimm* (1886), which included the story of "The Six Swans," used in this book; *The Baby's Own Aesop* (1886); and Oscar Wilde's *The Happy Prince and Other Tales* (1888), for which he made the drawing on page 117.

George Cruikshank (1792–1878) was born in London and became England's leading illustrator. It is said that Cruikshank was "the first who dared combine lively imagination and high good humor with fine drawing when he undertook to illustrate books for children." Indeed, his engravings for *German Popular Stories* (1823) are still looked upon as the first "modern" book illustrations for children, while the book itself is often referred to as the milestone that marked the beginning of the golden age of fairy-tale literature. "Rumpelstiltskin," illustrated on page 47, is taken from this book, which was the first translation of the Grimm Brothers' *Kinder- und Haus-Märchen*. Cruikshank's major work, however, was in the adult field. Among the hundreds of articles and books he illustrated were his own *Comic Alphabet* (1836); novels by Dickens,

157

George Cruikshank. From: *The History of Jack and the Beanstalk* (Bogue), 1853.

Ainsworth, Defoe, Irving, Goldsmith; plays by Shakespeare, Stowe's *Uncle Tom's Cabin* (1852), and Bunyan's *The Pilgrim's Progress* (1903). He also tried his hand—none too successfully—at rewriting some of the old fairy tales; it was Cruikshank's pictures that everybody always liked the best.

Gustave Doré (1833–1883) was an Alsatian, born in Strasbourg. At the early age of eleven his interest in lithography led him to study art, which in turn led him to Paris, where in 1848 he got his start on the *Journal pour rire*. By the 1850s he was a top name in his profession and exhibiting at the Salon. His success in France was later matched in London, where his work was popular enough for him to open his own Doré Gallery in 1858. Among the best-known books he illustrated are: Balzac's *Contes drolatiques* (1855); Dante's *Inferno* (1861); Cervantes' *The History of Don Quixote* (1863); Coleridge's *The Rime of the Ancient Mariner* (1865); Milton's *Paradise Lost* (1866); *Fables of La Fontaine* (1867); and *Fairy Tales Told Again* (1872), from which the engravings for "Puss in Boots" on pages 21–29 and "Sleeping Beauty" on pages 160–161 originated.

Richard Doyle. From: John Ruskin's *The King of the Golden River* (Smith, Elder), 1851.

Richard Doyle (1824–1883), the son of an Irish artist (and uncle of Sir Arthur Conan Doyle), was born in London, where, at the age of nineteen, he designed the famous first cover of *Punch*. In 1846 Doyle illustrated *The Fairy Ring* by the Grimm Brothers and Dickens' *The Cricket on the Hearth*. Between that year and 1871, he illustrated eighteen more books, notably Thackeray's *Rebecca and Rowena* (1850); Ruskin's *The King of the Golden River* (1851); Hughes's *Scouring of the White Horse* (1858); and *In Fairyland* (1870), which was the source for the illustrations in the Introduction to this book.

Gustav Doré. For: "Sleeping Beauty," from *Fairy Tales Told Again* (Cassell, Petter and Galpin), 1872. Photo: Courtesy the Pierpont Morgan Library.

Harry Clarke. For: "The Swineherd," from *Fairy Tales*
by Hans Christian Andersen (Harrap), 1916.

Kay Nielsen. From: *East of the Sun West of the Moon*
(Hodder & Stoughton), 1914.

Edmund Dulac. For: "Beauty and the Beast," from *Edmund Dulac's Fairy Book* (Hodder & Stoughton), 1916.

Edmund Dulac (1882–1953), a native of Toulouse, studied law before he decided to become an artist. This major decision landed him in the Toulouse Art School for three years, then in Paris for three months, and thereafter in London, where the Leicester Galleries recognized him first in 1907. By 1912 Dulac was a British subject. He painted, lectured, designed stage sets, stamps, and medals, did portraits, and illustrated numerous books, including *Stories from the Arabian Nights* (1907), which at once made him Arthur Rackham's main rival. Among the other books Dulac illustrated are: *The Rubáiyát of Omar Khayyám* (1909); *The Sleeping Beauty and Other Fairy Tales* (1910); *Stories from Hans Andersen* (1911), from which the color plate on page 48 is reproduced; *Poetical Works of Edgar Allan Poe* (1912); *Edmund Dulac's Fairy Book* (1916); and Hawthorne's *Tanglewood Tales* (1918).

Edmund Dulac. "Father Time." Watercolour from *The Studio* magazine, 1906.

Arthur Rackham. "The Man in the Wilderness." Painted for *Saint Nicholas* magazine.

Arthur Rackham. "The Gossips." Painted for *Saint Nicholas* magazine.

H. H. Emmerson. See Kate Greenaway.

Eugene Field (1850–1895) was born in St. Louis, Missouri, and became a journalist in his native city. He also worked in Kansas City and Denver before finally joining *The Chicago News* in 1853. Field's best-known poetry was published in *A Little Book of Western Verse* (1889), which included his "Wynken, Blynken, and Nod" and "Little Boy Blue," and in *Poems of Childhood* (1904), from which "The Sugar-Plum Tree" on page 145 is taken.

Henry Justice Ford (1860–1940). After graduating from Cambridge University, Ford studied at London's Slade School of Fine Art and, at the age of thirty-two, was exhibiting at the Royal Academy. As a book illustrator he is best known to most young readers for his drawings in *The Blue Fairy Book* (1889) and in all of the eleven subsequent fairy books in the Andrew Lang series. Ford's drawing on page 33 comes from "The Strong Prince" in *The Crimson Fairy Book* (1903).

Henry Justice Ford. For: "The Magic Ring," from *The Yellow Fairy Book* (Longmans, Green), 1894.

Kate Greenaway (1846–1901) was born in London, and studied drawing, she has told us, "at a class connected with the Kensington Art Schools." Her first major success was *Under the Window* (1879), which so caught the public's fancy that soon parents everywhere started dressing their children "in the Greenaway style." She illustrated well over eighty books, including her *Almanacs*. Other popular titles which she wrote or illustrated are: *The Kate Greenaway Birthday Book for Children* (1880); *A Day in a Child's Life*, with music by Miles Foster, and *Mother Goose*, both in 1881; *Little Ann and Other Poems*, written by Jane and Ann Taylor (1883); *Marigold Garden* (1885); *A Apple Pie*, and Bret Harte's *The Queen of the Pirate Isle*, both in 1886; Browning's *Pied Piper of Hamelin* (1888), from which her illustrations in this book are taken; and *The Kate Greenaway Book of Games* (1899).

   One of the best of Kate Greenaway's numerous imitators was H. H. Emmerson, whose charming illustration for J. G. Sowerby's rhyme on page 140 goes to show how great the Greenaway influence was in the 1880s.

The Grimm Brothers: Jacob (1785–1863) and *Wilhelm* (1786–1859), the orphan sons of a lawyer, grew up in Hesse, Germany, under the wing of a benevolent aunt who saw to it that they were "properly" educated. In 1812 the publication in Berlin of *Kinder- und Haus-Märchen,* a two-volume collection of local folk tales which the studious brothers had assembled orally and carefully written down over the years, became a milestone in fairy-tale literature. The first English translation, made by Edgar Taylor in 1823, was published in London as *German Popular Stories,* a single volume illustrated by the renowned George Cruikshank. Since then there have been dozens of new translations and adaptations of Grimm's fairy tales, and many hundreds of illustrated editions and "toy books."

Andrew Lang (1844–1912) was born in the Scottish border town of Selkirk and became well known as a historian and poet as well as an editor. He was brought up on the fairy tales of Perrault and Grimm, and today is probably best known, by children at least, as the editor of *The Blue Fairy Book* (1889) and the eleven other fairy books, each named after the color of its cloth binding. Somewhere between the "blue" and *The Lilac Fairy Book* (1910), which was the last in the series, Lang became known as "the undisputed king of the nursery book shelf." While he edited the books and contributed a Foreword to each, for the most part Mrs. Lang, with the collaboration of others, translated the fairy stories from many lands and languages.

Ethel Mars (who, like many a lady in her day, kept her birth date a deep secret) was a native of Springfield, Illinois, and was exhibiting at the Societé Nationale de Paris in 1907 Although primarily a painter (one of her portraits hangs in the Cincinnati Art Museum), Ethel Mars (or E. Mars as she is usually listed) is best known for her coloured wood block prints and for the illustrations she and M. H. Squire contributed to Robert Louis Stevenson's classic *A Child's Garden of Verses* (1900), from which her charming interpretation of his poem "The Wind" appears on page 143.

Kate Greenaway. From: her *Marigold Garden* (Routledge), 1885.

Ethel Mars. From: Stevenson's
A Child's Garden of Verses
(Russell), 1900.

Kay Nielsen (1886–1957) was born in Copenhagen. After deciding to make art his career, he moved to Paris in 1904, studied in the schools of Montparnasse, and remained in France until 1911, the year he was given a black-and-white show in London. He stayed on in England for five years, painting, designing, and doing illustration work. In 1913, when *In Powder and Crinoline* was published, the Leicester Galleries exhibited the original Nielsen illustrations. By 1917 he was exhibiting in New York, after which he was lured back to his native Denmark, where he designed sets for the Theatre Royal in Copenhagen. After two more exhibitions in London, Nielsen moved to America in 1939, settled in Hollywood, and designed sets and acted bit parts in films. His much-sought-after books include: *In Powder and Crinoline*, a collection of classic fairy tales edited by Sir Arthur Quiller-Couch (from which the illustrations for "The Twelve Dancing Princesses" between pages 81 and 89 are taken); *East of the Sun West of the Moon*, edited by P. C. Asbjörnsen and J. I. Moe in 1914 (see colour plate, page 163); *Old Tales from the North* (1919); Hans Andersen's *Fairy Tales* (1924); Grimm's *Hansel and Gretel* (1925); and Romer Wilson's *Red Magic* (1930).

Maxfield Parrish (1870–1966), a native of Philadelphia, graduated from Haverford College in 1891 and spent the next three years at the Pennsylvania Academy of Fine Art. During these student years one of his paintings was accepted for an exhibition at the Philadelphia Art Club. In 1895 the first of the almost uncountable number of magazine illustrations to be executed by Parrish appeared on the Easter-issue cover of *Harper's Bazar*. While continuing to paint, design murals, posters, advertisements, and do commercial illustrations for *Century Magazine, Collier's, Everybody's Magazine, Hearst's Magazine*, the *Illustrated London News*, the *Ladies' Home Journal, Life, St. Nicholas, Scribners' Magazine*, and others, Parrish also found time for books. Particularly well known are his illustrations in Kenneth Grahame's *The Golden Age* (1899) and *Dream Days* (1902); Eugene Field's *Poems of Childhood* (1904), from which the color plate on page 144 is taken; *The Arabian Nights, Their Best Known Tales*, edited by Kate Douglas Wiggin and Nora A. Smith in 1909; and Louise Saunders' *The Knave of Hearts* (1925).

Charles Perrault (1628–1703). To this distinguished Frenchman goes the major credit for turning the fairy tale—hitherto an oral tradition—into literature. This happened with the publication of his *Histoires ou contes du temps passé* in 1697. Among the tales Perrault recorded are "Sleeping Beauty" and "Puss in Boots" (both to be found in this book), "Little Red Riding Hood," "Bluebeard," "Diamonds and Toads," and "Hop o' My Thumb." Perrault was a member of the Académie Française and a retired civil servant when he undertook this historic work. It became a major success, artistically and commercially, from the very first moment it was published.

Howard Pyle (1853–1911) was born in Wilmington, Delaware, where he lived to create well over 3000 illustrations that found their way into the printed page. The first of his drawings to be reproduced anywhere appeared in *Scribner's Monthly* during 1876. Since then Pyle's reputation grew and grew, until by the 1890s he was no longer merely referred to as a great artist but was considered "an American institution." He painted, taught art, wrote articles, novels, and popular adventure tales for children too. He illustrated what he wrote, furthermore, and frequently was commissioned to do the same for other authors' stories. Fully a third of his illustrations and half of what he wrote were designed for the young reader. Among his many classics enjoyed by generations of young readers are: *The Merry Adventures of Robin Hood* (1883); *Pepper and Salt* (1886); *The Wonder Clock* (1887), from which the story of "Bearskin" has been chosen for this book; *Men of Iron* (1891); *The Story of King Arthur and His Knights* (1903); and *The Book of Pirates* (1921).

Maxfield Parrish. For: "The Reluctant Dragon," from Grahame's *Dream Days* (John Lane), 1902.

Arthur Rackham (1867–1939) was born in Lewisham, London, and studied at the Lambeth School of Art prior to 1885, when he started earning his bread and butter as a clerk in an insurance office. A year later he was delighted to find one of his paintings accepted by the Royal Academy. In 1892, having abandoned the world of insurance in favor of the world of art, Rackham became a staff artist on the *Westminster Budget*. Three years later an edition of Washington Irving's *Tales of a Traveller* was published for which he had made the illustrations. This was his first book, but interestingly enough it was his second attempt at illustrating Washington Irving—the story of *Rip Van Winkle*—that put Arthur Rackham's name in the limelight. That was in 1905. After that he rapidly developed into the most consistently successful illustrator of the new century. Few, if any, artists have illustrated fantasy so well as Rackham, or made it equally inviting to adults as to children. Among his best works are: *Fairy Tales of the Brothers Grimm* (1900, 1907), from which three selections appear in this book; Barrie's *Peter Pan in Kensington Gardens* (1906); *The Ingoldsby Legends*, and *Alice's Adventures in Wonderland*, both in 1907; Shakespeare's *A Midsummer Night's Dream* (1908); Wagner's *The Rhinegold and the Valkyrie* (1910) and *Siegfried and the Twilight of the Gods* (1911); *Aesop's Fables* (1912); *Mother Goose* (1913); Dickens' *A Christmas Carol* (1915); *Cinderella* (1919); *The Sleeping Beauty* (1920). Among the popular later Rackhams are: Goldsmith's *The Vicar of Wakefield* (1929); Andersen's *Fairy Tales* (1932); and his last book, Grahame's *The Wind in the Willows* (1940). See colour plates pages 166–67.

William Heath Robinson (1872–1944) was born at Hornsey Rise, London. He studied at the Islington School of Art and the Royal Academy School, specializing in fine art and landscape painting until, at the recommendation of his older brothers, Tom and Charles, he turned his attentions to the more lucrative work of illustration and advertising, just as they had done. Heath Robinson is especially remembered today for his wonderfully humorous drawings of ingenious but completely impractical contrivances. But between 1897 and 1944, when he illustrated more than fifty books, his genius was almost evenly divided between serious and light-hearted subjects as, for example: Bunyan's *The Pilgrim's Progress* (1897); *Fairy Tales from Hans Christian Andersen* (1899), the source of the two drawings for "The Swineherd" used in this book; *The Poems of Edgar Allan Poe* (1900); the humorous *Adventures of Uncle Lubin* (1902); Kipling's *The Dead King* (1910); his own *Bill the Minder* (1912); and Shakespeare's *A Midsummer Night's Dream* (1914).

Robert Louis Stevenson (1850–1894) was born in Edinburgh and grew up to become one of the leading essayists, novelists, and poets of his century. His most noted works for the younger reader include his great masterpiece, *Treasure Island* (1883); *A Child's Garden of Verses* (1885), from which the poem on page 142 was taken; and *Kidnapped* (1886).

Oscar Wilde (1854–1900) was born in Dublin, the son of an Irish doctor. After specializing in the classics at Trinity College, he continued his studies at Oxford, where he won the Newdigate Prize for his long poem *Ravenna* in 1878. Thereafter he did nothing to discourage his growing reputation as England's leading "aesthete." He was married in 1884 and four years later published *The Happy Prince and Other Tales*, which his children—and millions of others—grew up to love. Wilde's best-selling novel was *The Picture of Dorian Gray* (1891); his two most notable plays, *Lady Windermere's Fan* (1892) and *The Importance of Being Earnest* (1895).

Howard Pyle. From: *The Wonder Clock* (Harper), 1887.

W HEATH ROBINSON

Acknowledgements

Special thanks are due to the following for their valuable help and courtesies: the estate of Arthur Rackham; George G. Harrap & Co. Ltd. for the use of the Harry Clarke illustrations; Hodder & Stoughton Ltd. for permission to reproduce the Kay Nielsen and Edmund Dulac illustrations; Constable and Co. Ltd. for the material from *Fairy Tales of the Brothers Grimm*; Harper & Row, Publishers, for Howard Pyle's story of "Bearskin"; J. M. Dent & Co. for Heath Robinson's illustrations; and Frederick Warne & Co. for the Kate Greenaway illustrations.

I am also deeply indebted to Charles Pick, Nigel Viney, and Judith Elliott of William Heinemann Ltd.; Irene Whalley and the Victoria and Albert Museum, London, from whose collection of books the Edmund Dulac illustration for "The Princess and the Peas" and the illustrations by E.V.B. for "Thumbelina" were photographed; Gerald Gottlieb, Mrs. Evelyn Semler, and the Pierpont Morgan Library, New York, from whose collection of books the Doré illustrations for "Puss in Boots," the Cruikshank illustration for "Rumpelstiltskin," and the Charles Bennett illustrations to *Aesop's Fables* were photographed; Justin B. Schiller; Milton Reiseman; and to all the talented staff of Studio Books at Viking Penguin.

The other sources from which the material in this book has been taken are: Page 2: Illustration from *A New Child's Play* by E.V.B. [Eleanor Vere Boyle]. London: Sampson Low, Marston, Searle and Rivington, 1879. Pages 7–12: Illustrations from *In Fairyland: A Series of Pictures of the Elf-World by Richard Doyle with a Poem by William Allingham*. London: Longmans, Green and Co., 1875. Pages 13–20: Translation by Andrew Lang from *The Yellow Fairy Book*. London: Longmans, Green and Co., 1894. Illustrations from *Fairy Tales by Hans Christian Andersen*. Illustrated by E.V.B. [Eleanor Vere Boyle]. Newly translated by H. L. D. Ward and Augusta Plesner. London: Sampson Low, Marston, Low and Searle, 1872. Pages 21–29: Translation by Dinah Maria Craik from *The Fairy Book*. London: Thomas Nelson and Sons, 1863. Illustrations from *Fairy Tales Told Again* by Gustave Doré. London: Cassell, Petter and Galpin, 1872. Pages 30–33: From *The Crimson Fairy Book*. Edited by Andrew Lang, with illustrations by H. J. Ford. London: Longmans, Green & Co., 1903. Pages 34–45: Translation by Dinah Maria Craik from *The Fairy Book*. London: Thomas Nelson and Sons, 1863. Illustrations from *Beauty and the Beast*. An Old Tale New-Told, with Pictures by E.V.B. [Eleanor Vere Boyle]. London: Sampson Low, Marston, Low and Searle, 1875. Pages 46–47: Translation by Dinah Maria Craik from *The Fairy Book*. London: Thomas Nelson and Sons, 1863. Illustrations by George Cruikshank from *German Popular Stories*. Translated from *Kinder und Haus-Märchen*. Collected by M. M. Grimm, from Oral Tradition. London: C. Baldwyn, 1823. Pages 48–49: Translation by Charles Boner from *A Danish Story-Book*. London: Joseph Cundall, 1846. Illustrations by Edmund Dulac from *Stories from Hans Andersen*. London: Hodder & Stoughton, 1911. Pages 50–57: From *The Wonder Clock* by Howard Pyle. New York: Harper and Brothers, 1888. Pages 58–62: From *Household Stories*, *from the Collection of the Bros. Grimm*. Translated from the German by Lucy Crane; and Done into Pictures by Walter Crane. London: Macmillan and Company, 1886. Pages 63–68: Transla-

Heath Robinson. From: Shakespeare's *A Midsummer Night's Dream* (Constable), 1914.

tion by Dinah Maria Craik from *The Fairy Book*. London: Thomas Nelson & Sons, 1863. Illustration from "The Frog Prince" in Walter Crane's *Goody Two Shoes' Picture Books*. London and New York: George Routledge and Sons, 1875. Pages 69–80: From *Fairy Tales of the Brothers Grimm*. A New Translation by Mrs. Edgar Lucas, with Illustrations by Arthur Rackham. London: Freemantle & Co., 1900 (with colour plates from the revised edition of 1909 published by Constable and Co. Ltd., London). Pages 81–89: Translation by Andrew Lang from *The Red Fairy Book*. London: Longmans, Green and Co., 1890. Illustrations from *In Powder and Crinoline: Old Fairy Tales*. Retold by Sir Arthur Quiller-Couch. Illustrated by Kay Nielsen. London: Hodder & Stoughton, 1913. Pages 90–98: Translation by Dinah Maria Craik from *The Fairy Book*. London: Thomas Nelson & Sons, 1863. Illustrations from *Cinderella*, retold by C. S. Evans and illustrated by Arthur Rackham. London: William Heinemann, 1919. Pages 99–103: Translation by Andrew Lang from *The Yellow Fairy Book*. London: Longmans, Green and Co., 1894. Illustrations from *Fairy Tales from Hans Christian Andersen*. Illustrations by Tom, Charles, and William Heath Robinson. London: J. M. Dent & Sons, 1899. Pages 104–108: From *Fairy Tales of the Brothers Grimm*. A New Translation by Mrs. Edgar Lucas, with Illustrations by Arthur Rackham. London: Freemantle & Co., 1900 (with the colour plate from the revised edition of 1909 published by Constable & Co. Ltd., London). Pages 109–112: From *Household Stories, from the Collection of the Bros. Grimm*. Translated from the German by Lucy Crane; and Done into Pictures by Walter Crane. London: Macmillan and Company, 1886. Pages 113–119: From *The Happy Prince and Other Tales* by Oscar Wilde. Illustrated by Walter Crane and Jacob Hood. London: David Nutt, 1888. Pages 120–127: After M. Charles Marelles's "The Pied Piper" ("The Ratcatcher") in *The Red Fairy Book*. Edited by Andrew Lang. London: Longmans, Green & Co., 1890. Illustrations from *The Pied Piper of Hamelin* by Robert Browning. Illustrated by Kate Greenaway. London and New York: George Routledge and Sons, 1888. Pages 128–134: From *Fairy Tales by Hans Christian Andersen*. Illustrated by Harry Clarke. London: George Harrap & Co., 1916. Pages 135–139: From Randolph Caldecott's Picture Books: *Hey Diddle Diddle, the Cat and the Fiddle; Ride a Cock-Horse; A Frog He Would A-Wooing Go*. London and New York: George Routledge & Sons, 1883–1885. Page 140: From *Afternoon Tea*. Rhymes for Children by J. G. Sowerby and H. H. Emmerson. London: Frederick Warne & Co., 1880. Page 141: From *Marigold Garden*. Pictures and rhymes by Kate Greenaway. London and New York: George Routledge and Sons, 1885. Pages 142–143: From *A Child's Garden of Verses* by Robert Louis Stevenson. Illustrated by E. Mars and M. H. Squire. New York: R. H. Russell, 1900. Pages 144–145: From *Poems of Childhood* by Eugene Field with Illustrations by Maxfield Parrish. New York: Charles Scribner's Sons, 1904.

Decoration by Kay Nielsen